IF SUSIE SAID JUMP

Karen Powell was brought up in Rochester and studied English at Lucy Cavendish College, Cambridge. She lives in York. This is her second novel.

If Susie Said Jump

KAREN POWELL

Harbour

Extract from 'Ithaka' by C. P. Cavafy
translated by Edmund Keeley & Philip Sherrard
reprinted by kind permission of Chatto & Windus

Extract from *The Cantos* of Ezra Pound
reprinted by kind permission of Faber & Faber

Harbour Books Ltd
20 Castlegate
York YO1 9RP
www.harbourbooks.co.uk

Represented in Great Britain & Ireland by
Signature Book Services
First published in Great Britain by
Harbour Books 2006
Copyright © Karen Powell 2006

A catalogue record for this book is
available from the British Library.
ISBN 13: 978 1905128 06 8
ISBN 10: 1905128 06 1

Typeset by Antony Gray
Printed and bound in Finland by WS Bookwell

ITHAKA

As you set out for Ithaka
hope your road is a long one,
full of adventure, full of discovery.
Laistrygonians, Cyclops,
angry Poseidon – don't be afraid of them:
you'll never find things like that on your way
as long as you keep your thoughts raised high,
as long as a rare excitement
stirs your spirit and your body.
Laistrygonians, Cyclops,
wild Poseidon – you won't encounter them
unless you bring them along inside your soul,
unless your soul sets them up in front of you.

C. P. Cavafy

My mother calls me into the living-room and I stand in the doorway, resentful at being summoned – at the way she beckons with her hand but does not take her eyes away from the screen of our portable television.

'Watch,' she says, still not looking at me, or at Hannah, who is building a neat Lego house on the carpet at my mother's feet. 'They're showing it again.' I stand in the middle of the room, following her gaze towards the television, see a vast, brightly lit arena that turns dark with banks of people at the edges and, in the middle, standing before a pair of bars, a tiny figure with long, spindly legs. She is wearing a white leotard with coloured vertical stripes down the side of it and she is rubbing chalk into her hands, her eyes dark, inward-looking. She seems to be waiting for something. Then, in response to a signal from something – someone – beyond the range of the camera, she raises a hand above her head and the next moment she is airborne, spinning like a Catherine wheel around that pair of bars, whipping her small body this way and that between them, every movement making the next seem the only possible sequel. She works efficiently, faster and faster, towards something unstoppable, and suddenly, when her momentum makes it impossible to do anything else, she unpeels her hands from the bars and soars up towards that white glare of lights. My mother, though she has already seen this once, gasps, and every person in that silent arena forgets to breathe until the small figure has turned through the air and then, almost casually, as an afterthought, she plants her feet back upon the ground.

The silence lasts a second longer and then the stadium explodes with flashlights and an inhuman roar. The girl's face remains impassive – dark eyes expressionless as the camera zooms in upon her – but the proud curve of her muscular-chested little body, arms stretched high above her head to signal the completion of the exercise, tells us there was no doubt in her mind that she could do what she has just done.

Nadia Comaneci's first perfect score of the 1976 Olympics – which was to be followed by another six in the coming days – released a kind of yearning in me that summer, something wild and adventurous that must have been waiting there all along, waiting to break through the surface of my little girls' games and a seemingly placid nature. Now I saw that it was possible to be something more than I was already, a thought which had never occurred to me before, and this new idea grew, a restless excitement stirring within me, and with it came something else too, a dissatisfaction with what I saw as ordinary life, of hours wasted just being the same as you'd always been. Now I understood that I too must be perfect, and in precisely the same way as my heroine, there could be no inbetweens, no compromises. And so I left my books and my dolls behind, the company of children who were prepared to do a few handstands against the presbytery wall at the end of the street but who soon tired of my relentlessness, and I began to practise gymnastics every day of that drought-stricken summer. I practised at home in the garden, on the parched lawn, the grass burnt biscuit-brown by the sun, where only my family could witness my first stiff efforts, and then, when the new school year began, every lunchtime and playtime, on a small strip of grass at the edge of the playground. A man on the television said Nadia Comaneci was first spotted turning cartwheels in the schoolyard and, though all this happened in a far-off country called Romania, with mountains and an Iron Curtain – something I imagine to be like the heavy contraption the dinner ladies pull across the serving area once they finish serving food in the school hall, a kind of sliding, concertinaed door running through the middle of fields, down city streets – I honestly believed that the same thing might happen to me, that I too might be whisked out of a life that felt too commonplace for me now.

My mother, seeing that this was not just another one of my passing fancies, sent me along to a local gymnastics club that autumn, and it was there, with proper tuition and in the company of twenty or so other little girls and boys, that my body began to do what I wanted it to do, where I learnt to hold a handstand in mid-air and then slowly let the weight of my legs tip me farther until first one leg then the other found the floor, learnt how to pull myself out of this position with a graceful, flowing curve or else a quick, muscular snap. I learned, too, how to flip myself over backwards or to slide down into the splits and make grown-ups wince, learned to trust my hands and feet to seek out the four-inch width of the balance beam, eschewing the expanses of air either side of that varnished yellow strip of wood. Every week we pushed our bodies into new shapes, and if we weren't making sufficient progress, we would have to sit in a line with our backs against the wall, pull our legs in towards our chests and then place the soles of our feet together, each of us trying to push our knees down towards the ground in a butterfly shape. The teacher would move along the line observing our efforts and then stand upon the knees of each child, one by one, forcing us into still greater suppleness.

Before long, I was ready for competitions. You stand, poised, at one end of a line of pushed-together mats, waiting for the nod from the teacher who is stationed to one side of the wooden vault at the far end of the room. Out of the corner of your eye you are aware of the row of little girls and boys in leotards and shorts sitting cross-legged to one side of you. They are waiting their turn, legs blotched with the cold that strikes up through the floor of the church hall. On the other side, you feel the rustle of the audience, cobbled together from mothers and fathers, brothers, sisters, grandparents, sitting on the metal chairs that are normally stacked up along one wall of the room. You take no notice of them, their coughs and shuffles. You remind yourself of Nadia's solemn, inward demeanour and you are more determined than ever never to become a dancing, waving puppet of a gymnast, a crowd-pleaser like Olga Korbut. You see people smile at your seriousness. Notice the trestle table laid out with cups and saucers and plates of cakes by the kitchen hatch. You raise a hand, keeping your eyes straight ahead, lean back on one heel, letting both arms swing behind you now, take a long, determined breath and then you are off, bare feet pounding over the mats, pushing off those cool spongy surfaces, a blue sea beneath your toes, knowing instinctively to avoid the gaps and your legs are coming up to your chest now, faster and faster as you hurtle towards the vault. Then you hit the springboard and it is too late to stop, even if you wanted to, head dropping as you launch yourself forwards, hands reaching for the surface of the vault – padded, beige suede, the nap worn shiny – body following of its own accord now, beginning to rise behind you. The vault rocks on its base with the impact. You release all the power that is coiled up in your small arms, make it surge through all of you and you are spinning through a blurred jumble of colour, the protesting squawk of a baby from somewhere in the audience, the wild streak of strip lights. A shiny blue crash mat looms up, ready to save you and the teacher and her assistant are right there as usual, one on either side of the vault, waiting to catch you if you've miscalculated the whole manoeuvre or, with a hand in the small of your back, to propel you forwards if you have under-rotated. But I did not want them there, knew that I would *never* need them there, because inside of me was a kind of magic, making my body know precisely what to do, without any need for external assistance, any thought of rescue. Once, when I was a child, I knew how to launch myself into unknown air and to land perfectly every time.

CHAPTER 1

I cannot prevent a little moan of terror escaping me as the plane lurches up into the sky. I clutch Joe's arm but cannot speak, just keep staring down at the book in my lap, knowing that I will not be capable of anything while the plane is pointing itself up to the heavens at an angle so hubristic it demands to be flung back down to earth. Fortunately, there is no turbulence once we have cleared the clouds and after some minutes the reassuringly cultured voice of the pilot announces that we have reached cruising height. I watch anxiously as a stewardess prepares to bring round the drinks' trolley, a hot waft of warming food reaching us from the galley behind her. Joe catches her eye and she comes down the aisle to him, bends over him and then nods, glancing across at me. The pilot comes on again, starts telling us about today's flying conditions which are, mercifully, good, and a few moments later the stewardess returns, bringing me a can of orange juice and a miniature bottle of vodka though drinks are not yet being served to the rest of the cabin.

'Are you all right?' she asks, eyes kind beneath sharp wings of green eye shadow, and I manage to smile while Joe pours the vodka and orange juice into a plastic cup and the captain chats on about the countries and cities over which we will be flying. I sip my drink slowly, picturing in my mind a map of Europe – of the kind I might find in the pocket of the seat in front of me when I am brave enough to move – a map with curving route markers, confidently joining one place to another, and it is comforting to realise that we are nosing forward along one of those solid red lines right now, no longer just careering blindly up into the sky. I stare out the window, the warmth of the vodka slinking through me, watch the pure morning sun glinting off another aeroplane which is skimming lightly over the clouds in the far distance. Joe points out of the window to the right of me: the end of land. Beneath us, the viscous grey of the English Channel.

*　　*　　*

I interrupt Joe at his crossword. 'I can hardly believe it, going back after all this time. It's odd,' I say.

He looks up at me questioningly, his pen in mid-air, weighing up this wonderment. He never quite trusts these sudden fervours of mine, especially since they usually arrive when I am at my most downcast or fearful. 'People do,' he says lightly.

A meal comes and goes and then I read for a while, skirt around the edges of the crossword that Joe has abandoned, before giving up and looking out of the window instead, feeling a growing sense of anticipation as I watch the neat patterned fields of France slip away beneath us, wait for the foothills of the Alps to swell the ground. They come, and soon there are sharp pyramids of snow on mountaintops, and roads running like thread through deep valleys, along crags and beside glittering lakes. Joe is leaning against my shoulder now. The little furrow between his eyebrows does not smooth itself out, even in sleep. He is breathing heavily in my ear and I close my eyes then, let myself drift for a little while, though I never lose awareness of the thrumming of the engines vibrating through the body of the aeroplane, become even more alert, if that is possible, to the unnaturalness of my position, held here between heaven and earth by nothing more than a tight skin of metal.

*　　*　　*

On the other side of the Alps, there are no more green fields and neat towns and villages, just mile after mile of hard brown land, pale tracks through the dry earth, the occasional gleam of a railway track and meagre scatterings of civilisation, like handfuls of rubble thrown from a giant's hand. I close my eyes again, dream a little – of work, of home – and I only just awake in time to capture the moment I have been waiting for all along, as we leave the brown rock of the Balkans behind and slide out, at last, over the improbable, cartoon blue of the Ionian Sea.

*   *   *

'Christ, it's hot!' says a man behind me as we leave the plane. I turn to see him peeling off a tracksuit top, his expression half-frightened. He is right: behind the stiff breeze, which pulls at our clothes and whips my hair across my face, is something immense. We wait in a queue outside the terminal building, everyone rooting out sunglasses to counteract the white glare. Someone has left a half-empty bottle of lemonade on a low wall. A wasp has found its way inside, is drowning now in the warm yellowy liquid, shuddering towards a sweet suffocating death. I had forgotten what it feels like, this merciless midday heat, have to remind myself how, after a few days, you adjust to it, learn to slow yourself down to the donkey's pace of the Mediterranean. Till then it can feel as though something inexorable and damaging has been visited upon you. The airport terminal is cool enough though. It looks brand new: all darkened glass, air-conditioning and stony-faced officials in mirrored sunglasses. We wait for our luggage and Joe risks a cigarette, despite the prominent no-smoking signs, because, as he points out, none of the Greeks seem to be paying them any attention. Then we bypass the phalanx of reps wearing nylon short-sleeved blouses and tight welcome smiles in the arrival area and step out into the heat again.

You cannot miss Will's broad figure, his height. He is standing on the far side of the road – away from the chaos of taxis and luggage trolleys and the haze of exhaust fumes from coach engines – leaning against a silver people-carrier. Rising up behind him, beyond the plain on which the airport is situated, is a rocky, unforgiving landscape. He sees us almost immediately and steps forwards, but Joe motions to him to stay where he is, that we will come to him. Will's arm stays raised in greeting for a second longer and for an odd moment, as we step out from under the canopy of the terminal into an explosion of light, there seems something ineffably desolate about that hand stretching upwards in the blue of the sky, the thickness of the forearm and the solidity of fingers made insubstantial by that harsh backdrop, turned almost transparent by a trick of the light. Adrift in a strange land, I think.

'Milly's suddenly decided she has heatstroke, so I thought Susie'd better stay behind with her,' explains Will, heaving my suitcase into the boot. Detecting, perhaps, disappointment in my expression, he smiles. 'Also, I think Susie wanted to be waiting for you at the villa.'

'Yes,' I say, understanding then that the airport might be too prosaic a meeting place. Joe lifts the second suitcase in and allows Will to slam the door shut. Samuel is sitting in the third row of seats inside the car. Joe taps on the window and gives him a thumbs-up. He peers out at us and then the glass swims over his face as he puts the window down and manages a wide-eyed greeting. The less robust of Susie and Will's children, Samuel looks even paler and more gangly limbed than when I last saw him. I lean in and kiss him on the cheek and I cannot tell if this pleases or disconcerts him. By the time Joe and I are sitting in our seats, he has returned to his book. Will jumps into the front seat and starts the engine, the air-conditioning roars into life, battling against the blanket of hot air that has already found its way into the car while the doors and windows have been open.

We negotiate our way past the taxis and the line of coaches, each with a board propped up in the windscreen announcing the name of its destination, and then we are on a coastal road, passing through little resorts with shops bright with lilos and beach footballs and racks of postcards, and people in shorts and sarongs sitting at plastic tables beneath umbrellas. I shift in my seat, uncomfortable in the heavy denim of my jeans and a cotton shirt that feels too tight beneath my arms. Already I envisage them thrown aside in the bottom of a wardrobe where they will remain for the rest of the holiday. Joe is sitting in the passenger seat, next to Will, talking in the way that men who share similar backgrounds – university and a passing interest in sport – fall into readily, a loose, non-committal way of speaking, suggestive of an easy camaraderie that doesn't necessarily exist.

'Have you been having a good time, Samuel?' I say, turning in my seat. 'Mummy said the villa has a lovely swimming-pool.'

'I can't swim yet,' he says, looking up from his book. 'The villa's OK though,' he adds politely.

Joe points out the island's capital to our left. I lean forward, look over his shoulder at the map he is studying, and see that it is situated on a peninsula and not on a separate piece of land as you might assume from here. Will tells us that it was destroyed by an earthquake in the fifties but it looks pretty enough from where we are and there is something uplifting about the wide stretch of blue water that sparkles between here and there and the narrow road bridge that crosses it. The road turns inland, where there is little to see, and then we are back out on the coast again. There are mountains in the distance, a kind of ominous swelling on the horizon. I feel a little cowed by them after the green neatness of England, and by the scale of the great bays we are skirting, where other cars, farther ahead, are little more than a glint of sun on metal against a vast, unremitting canvas of rock. I stare out of the window, say little. Though the lettering on the road signs is Greek and the smatterings of language I heard around me at the airport, pebbly and guttural, were instantly familiar, this is not yet a Greece that I know

'Mount . . . ' I hear snatches of what Will is saying ' . . . the highest on the island. Famous for its fir trees . . . which, so they say, were used for the ships in the Trojan War . . . '

It strikes me that for someone who has only been on the island for two days, Will seems to know a good deal about the place. If you'd only just met him – hadn't known him when he was younger and only just growing into himself – you could easily mistake this mantle of affable, public-school kind of confidence he wears for the real thing, might even take against him for it. Joe is flipping through the guidebook, talking in the over-animated manner he slips into when he wants to be perceived as an enthusiast. I rebuke myself for the thought, remind myself that Joe's bursts of energy are not a mark of insincerity on his part, more a return to an older form of himself. I rest my hand on his shoulder as a token of contrition and, at the same time, a reminder to him that I am here, right behind him – but it is a futile gesture because you can't reach him when he is like this, seeking the approbation of others.

'Here we are!'

Will has turned sharply, leaving the main road for a dirt track. The car slews slightly and I get a quick glimpse of a metal sign tacked to a tree trunk, an arrow beneath pointing away from the main road, but there is no time to read it as Will accelerates along the track, orange-brown dust rising around us.

'Could have done with a bloody four-wheel drive rather than this thing,' says Will cheerily, swerving to avoid a pothole. We continue up the rough track for a minute or two more, climbing higher and higher away from the main road which lies beneath us now. We are travelling towards a point where the land seems to fall away and the sky begins and I can see nothing up there ahead of us, no more than a clutch of trees among the rough rock, and, even though it would be ludicrous to do so, I have an urge to ask Will if he is sure about this. Joe winds down his window and there is no noise up here but the electric whine of cicadas in the dry foliage that catches at the car as we pass. Then, when it looks as if we can go no farther without tumbling into the sky, we turn a corner, swing round a stand of umbrella pines on to a suddenly smooth driveway and there in front of us, floating against a blue sky, and looking as if it is only anchored to this crag of land by the vines growing up its yellow walls, is the Villa Stamatia.

CHAPTER 2

Susie must have been listening for us. She appears from somewhere – not the house – and walks across the driveway towards us, her pace increasing as she comes. She is lightly dressed, in flip-flops and a bright-blue cotton kaftan, but in the glare of the afternoon sun she looks out of her element. For a second I am disconcerted and then it comes to me as a surprise, the realisation that Susie's kind of beauty – pale and fine like Joe's – is more suited to the grey, nuanced light of Northern Europe. She hugs Joe and drops a kiss on his cheek and then turns to me.

'You're here!' she smiles, arms spread as if in wonder, a gesture that does not quite belong to her. She links an arm through mine: 'Thank the Lord – we're going mad for adult company already.'

'This place!' I say, motioning to the villa, its setting, high above the world. 'I had no idea from the photos.'

'Yes, I was meant to forward some more, wasn't I?' Her eyes follow where I have gestured and she smiles again, looking at me expectantly.

'Can I go down to the pool?' interrupts Samuel. His mother nods, slides a hand over his hair without looking down at him.

'How's Milly?' I ask, looking around for her. 'Will said she wasn't feeling well.'

'Oh, doing her best to be a complete little bitch as usual,' says Susie drawing me across the driveway. The tone is throwaway, the words typically Susie, but still they shock me because Milly is a sweet-faced girl with auburn hair, the colour of her father's, curling to her shoulders. Susie sees my expression and pulls a face.

'Come on!' she says, following Will and Joe, who are carrying our luggage up the steps towards the villa. 'Come and look at everything.'

We inspect our own room first which, even though it is shuttered against the midday heat, is airy and light. It is to the left of the hallway, which is marble-floored and almost the width of a room itself. Then Susie takes us from room to room, Joe and I remarking upon the understated opulence of the villa as we go. Will and Susie's bedroom and the children's lead off from the main living area, where there are caramel-coloured sofas, a long low coffee table and sliding doors out on to a canopied sun-terrace. Through an archway is a large kitchen and utility room, where plates decorated with simple Greek designs hanging on the walls are the only nod towards rusticity.

'But you'll want to unpack now,' says Susie, coming to a sudden halt, just as our fervency is beginning to sound over-sustained. 'Come and find us by the pool when you're done.' And she leaves us alone to settle into our room, flip-flops slapping on the marble floor of the hallway as she goes.

*   *   *

The minute you move outside you feel the exposure. The house is built on concrete columns, with a garage or store-room beneath the sun terrace and steps leading up to the front door. Joe, who finished unpacking some minutes before I did, is sitting in a sheltered spot at the bottom of these steps, but up here, where the wind sighs all around you, sliding over the clean new walls and windows of this villa as if they hardly exist, snagging only for a moment among the dwarf rose-bushes planted along the edge of the sun terrace, there is nothing to hold you fast. I grasp the low concrete wall, remembering to wait for everything to settle again. Across the driveway, painted the same buttery yellow as the villa, is another wall, curving in a semi-circle and broken in one place by some steps leading down through the cypress trees. I hear the sound of splashing from somewhere below and a shriek of protest that might be Samuel's, and remember from the few photographs Susie managed to forward to me that the pool is set into a terrace on the hillside. To the right of the villa, beyond the driveway and the umbrella pines, the land falls away sharply. In the distance, I see white houses on a hillside, a deep bay and a jostle of boats in a small harbour. On the other side of the villa, there is another gap in the wall, narrower this time, leading to a steep, but negotiable-looking slope. A rough track curls down towards an olive grove and I recall Will saying something in the car about a small beach below the villa from which it is possible to swim. Joe stands up to join me. In this harsh sun his pale skin looks almost bruised, though he cannot have been waiting for me more than ten minutes or so. In a few days time, as always, he will surprise me by turning a deep brown.

*   *   *

It was Milly yelling, not Samuel, who is sitting on the edge of a rectangular, blue-tiled pool, scooping up water in his hands and grinning to himself.

'He's soaked me!' she protests as we emerge from the trees on to a terrace where hibiscus and bougainvillaea of an almost fluorescent pink range over grey stone walls and the hum of bees is shoulder-high. She hears us coming down the steps and turns. I cannot help but stare. It is almost a year since we last saw her and if I didn't recognise some quality in her voice I might be persuaded that the girl standing here in front of us isn't Milly at all. The child with the eager expression and ballet dancer's limbs is gone, swallowed up inside this heavy-set creature who, despite the heat, is dressed in black jeans, biker boots and a battered denim jacket. Milly's auburn curls have vanished, replaced by a black, glossless bowl of hair, shorter and spikier at the crown, which makes her newly-pudgy face seem even rounder.

'Perhaps he thought you needed cooling down,' says Susie in a sun-lazy voice, putting down a magazine. 'Aren't you going to say hello to Alice and Joe? Then you could go and change into something else.'

Milly glares at her mother and then at Samuel again.

'Hello,' she says, greeting us in a clear, sullen voice and then screwing up her eyes in exhaustion, as though doing so has cost her dearly. 'You're here,' she adds, an echo of her mother, and then turns away again. 'I'm going for a walk,' she announces to her parents.

'Good idea,' says Susie brightly. 'Come and have some wine, Alice – the agency left a few bottles in the fridge and they're actually . . . '

'Into town,' says Milly, interrupting.

'Which one? Or would you prefer beer, Joe?'

'How should I know? Wherever's nearest.' Milly does not move. Her eyes are black-rimmed with kohl and her heavy make-up looks hot and greasy in this light, sweat breaking through the matt surface of white powder across her nose.

'I told you yesterday,' replies Susie, with a small smile. 'There's nowhere within walking distance.'

Milly's made-up face has becomes a child's again, a wobbling mask of rage and disbelief. Susie glances at us, gives us a lightly apologetic smile. Will looks over the top of the book he is reading.

'You're seriously telling me I'm *stuck* here . . . With no one to talk to . . . ?' Milly raises her hands to her temples, looks around her in all directions in a parody of panic, and then out to sea, as if she is willing the yacht in the bay below to transform itself into a boatload of teenagers, come to rescue her from this fate. I resist the urge to smile at her performance.

'Well,' Susie sweeps her hand in the air, encompassing the villa up above us and the terrace where we are sitting, 'it's hardly a prison sentence, is it?'

Milly stares at her mother again, as if she would like to hit her. Then she looks as if she is about to cry. Joe, who always says he has had his fill of difficult children, is looking at Milly with open distaste.

Suddenly Will throws down his book and jumps up. 'Come on,' he orders, walking across to his daughter and putting his hand on her shoulder. 'Let's jump in the car and go to the supermarket in Aghia . . . whatever it's called. You can have a wander around the village for half an hour.'

'Let me come!' calls Samuel from the other end of the pool. 'I'm bored!' He is pigeon-chested and stick-limbed, his hips no more than two nubs above his swimming-trunks. Milly says nothing more, but follows her father up the steps. Samuel trots after them a second later, still hopping into his shorts.

'Ungrateful horrors, aren't they?' says Susie in equable tones. 'I don't think they know what they're supposed to *do* with this kind of holiday yet. They're used to having more organised for them.' She gets up from her sun-lounger and slips the blue kaftan over her bikini, pushes her feet into her flip-flops. 'I'll fetch another bottle, shall I?' Then, over her shoulder and grinning as she makes her way up the steps, 'Don't worry, Milly's only unbearable almost all the time.'

Joe waits till she is out of hearing.

'Christ, I'm not surprised they invited us here,' he says in a mock-whisper, sitting on the edge of a sun-lounger and squinting up at the sun. 'You'd want a buffer zone with Milly on the rampage, wouldn't you?' Out to sea, beyond the yacht, a larger boat – a ferry perhaps – hangs in the water. Behind it an island, or perhaps a promontory extending far out in the navy-blue water, its stony limbs stretching into the sea.

'Do you think that could be Ithaka over there?' I ponder, picturing a map in my head. 'You should be able see it from this side of the island.' Then: 'I guess Milly's just turned into a teenager.'

'It *was* all a bit last-minute,' persists Joe. 'Us being here at all, I mean.'

'Very Susie though,' I say. That phrase I have heard from other lips so often. I think of the phone-call that came out of nowhere. The hurried summons, some tale of an overbooking, of the Villa Stamatia being offered as an alternative to the original villa in Majorca or Minorca or wherever it was: a larger, more expensive property with nothing extra to pay.

'It's Greece,' she insisted. 'I'm not going without you.' And her knowing me too well to let me procrastinate, saying I had to decide then. Right then. 'Before Will gets involved and packs us all off to fucking Disneyland again. Or,' I can hear the shudder in her voice down the phone, 'invites someone vile from work along instead. You have to rescue me, Alice.'

'Well,' says Joe, stretching. 'I wouldn't be wholly surprised if we're only here to stop Milly murdering her own mother.' I get up and walk along the back of the terrace, sit down at the edge of the pool, letting my legs trail in the cool, beckoning water. I glance back at him, lying flat on the sun-lounger now, arms spread out, absorbing the sun. His words are harmless enough but they seem to have ushered in an ugliness where it does not belong. I remind myself that they come more from his habit of chipping away at things for the sake of doing so, than any real belief that Susie brought us here in a particular capacity.

The sun is hammering against my shoulders and the back of my neck. I lean out across the water, allowing myself to tip forwards little by little, prolonging the moment for as long as possible. I think of something else Joe hasn't accounted for in his half-hearted conspiracy theory: that it has always been me needing Susie and not the other way round; but his eyes are closed now, so I keep on leaning and then, when I am about to fall anyway, I push hard away from the tiles with the soles of my feet and let myself plunge, falling down through that perfect blue surface into a simpler world.

CHAPTER 3

In 1980 Elena Mukhina, star of the Russian gymnastics squad and winner of the 1978 World Championship women's all-round title, fell during a training session, shattering the vertebrae in her neck. News was slow to filter out from the Russian camp but in time it became known that Mukhina had fallen during a tumbling exercise and was paralysed from the neck down, would never walk, let alone compete, again. I do not know whether it was this, or the fact that, like my first heroine, the now veteran gymnast Nadia Comaneci, I was starting to lose my child's body, new weight dragging at my bones making it harder and harder for me to resist the pull of gravity, but by my twelfth birthday I had given up gymnastics for ever.

The following year my mother closed down her jewellery shop in the small artsy-craftsy Devonshire town where we lived, packed me, Hannah and all our things into her little car and drove eastwards, all the way to Daycliffe, a raw-faced provincial sprawl where she had taken a job teaching design at the local art college. We left behind Christian, my sister Hannah's father, also a teacher, whom I remember as a small, over-solicitous man who wore bicycle clips and a green tweed jacket with chalk-dust on the sleeves.

We spent that first summer crammed into a rented houseboat and then, just before the beginning of the new school year, we moved into a small terrace on Neville Street, with rooms looking out over a wind-blown cemetery to the rear and the concrete playground of Hannah's new junior school opposite our front door. My mother never showed any sign of regret for Christian, liked to joke in later years that he, in fact, turned out to be the least Christian person she'd ever known, judging by the rapidly dwindling number of maintenance payments and access visits he bothered to make. My sister sobbed inconsolably for two days after our departure and then seemed to forget about her father for the most part. But to me his absence seemed to echo that of my own father, whom I had never known (him being no more than a chance encounter that my mother had had in a hippy retreat on the island of Ios). With my new teenage sensibility I could not help working up the connection, fanning the flames of what I regarded secretly – and rather proudly – as tragedy at the centre of my life. In my mind, the moment when we left Christian and the safety of that little community behind us marked the time when our family fell out of kilter.

I suppose, then, I would not have considered myself a lucky person at that time, but in reality I must have been, because if it hadn't been for Susie arriving late that first day of the autumn term, flying into one of the classrooms – that already smelt of damp blazers and weak orange squash in Tupperware beakers – just as the register was being taken, and dropping down into the nearest free seat which just happened to be next to me, we might never have become friends.

Daycliffe Manor, where we met, was not a manor at all, just a square block, two storeys high, set up on a hill above the housing estates, 1930s' semis and Victorian terraces that fell down in tiers towards the town centre and the red-brick oblong of the multi-storey car park and shopping mall. From the school playing fields you could just see the wide grey curve of the river which might seem, from that distance, to promise some adventure, might even glint for a second through the thick haze of a rare, hot summer's day. But at closer hand, it turned out to be a sullen stretch of water, thick with mud at it edges and clogged up with warehouses, ancient rusting hulks and iron piers on the point of collapse. The school, built in the sixties to replace an older building on the site, was the colour of mould. In the centre there was a quad, reserved, apparently, for the teachers but always empty, with a bench on each side and a few sparse beds of roses that, notwithstanding the sheltered conditions, always looked bullied by the chill, watery winds that swept across the hockey pitch and the netball courts all winter long. In those winter months of the year, condensation dripped down the classroom walls, dampening the air and coating the windows in a permanent cold sweat.

I kept myself apart in my first few days, knowing no one and overwhelmed by the vast number of girls everywhere around me – so many compared with the small sedate classes of the village school I had left behind! They seemed to me like some kind of potentially violent force – propelling themselves along corridors and down stairwells each break time in twisting masses, like salmon pushing upstream, crashing bags of books and elbows against one another at the end of each day, yelling at each other in an accent that sounded brutal to my ears, stopping to hoik grey over-the-knee socks up over mottled legs. Right from the start, I sensed that my long, hippyish tangle of hair, my West Country accent – the *differentness* of me – would lead inevitably to exclusion, and so I didn't even think of offering myself up for approval to my classmates. I spoke only when spoken to and, realising that my ability to whip through my work with almost no effort (while the rest of the class were sighing with bemusement) would do nothing to endear me to them, I took to hiding myself away in the library, keeping my head down as much as I could.

Later, when Susie was in one of her fierce moods, she used to say that she was sick of people bothering her and perhaps it was this, as well as the empty seat beside me that first morning, that drew her to me, because certainly I would have never dreamed of bothering someone like her. Even from the beginning I could not miss the perpetual clamour around Susie, a clamour that I could surely not have infiltrated had I tried to do so – the gaggle of girls who trailed in her wake, drawn by her beauty (which, when I see it in the few photographs I have kept from this time, has a cool, peculiarly modern quality) and by the fearless charm that later enabled her to extract herself neatly from whatever cruelties she instigated against her elders to pass the long, empty afternoons of our school-days. Susie crawling beneath the desk to set fire to the science mistress's shoelaces and maintaining her innocence even after the matches were discovered in her blazer pocket . . . Susie throwing all the poster paints out of the art-room window, flirting outrageously with the nervous young English supply teacher, brushing up against him with her small breasts at every opportunity until his acne-scarred face was a perpetual, painful crimson . . .

In my favour, as far as Susie might have been concerned, was the fact that most of the other girls in our class lived on the edges of town and therefore travelled home on one of the double-decker buses that thrummed outside the school gates at 3.45 each day, while Susie and I lived within walking distance of the school, she with her parents and three sisters above the pub her parents ran, three streets away from us. It is hard to know, looking back, exactly how or why it happened, but what I remember is that even before my half-term had come and gone, Susie and I had shaken off most of the stragglers. And after that there were girls who drifted in and out of the picture from time to time, but really it was always just the two of us.

CHAPTER 4

On our first full day on the island, we drive down to the little fishing village along the coast for lunch. Afterwards, Will and Joe take the children to an ice-cream parlour and to buy wine for the evening, while Susie and I stay behind in the taverna, drinking cold retsina and stealing cigarettes from the packet Joe has left on the table.

'Where should we go, Al?' asks Susie.

'I'm not sure,' I say, flicking through Will's guidebook and wishing I had made more of an effort to research the island before we came. 'I'm not used to planning these things really. Not when I'm somewhere like this. My mother just used to hire a car, throw us in the back and drive out from wherever we were to see what we could find. But I'm not sure . . . ' I look at her doubtfully, unable to imagine Milly, or even Samuel, submitting to such a nebulous scheme.

Susie laughs, understanding what is left unspoken. 'No, you're right. The children would be hell. Will too, for all his enthusiasms. The idea of setting out somewhere without knowing where he was heading . . . ' She shakes her head, adds fiercely: 'I hate my family sometimes. They don't really get the *concept* of adventures.'

'It doesn't matter,' I say, looking down at the guidebook again. 'I'm sure I can find plenty in here.'

'You can't go anywhere with any of them,' says Susie, frowning to herself. 'I hate them.'

The next day we drive out again – 'Alice must decide where, not you!' says Susie, chiding Will, who is already chipping in with suggestions for amendments to the day I have planned. We visit some caves which Samuel seems to enjoy most, testing the echoes with falsetto shrieks, and then on to a monastery up in the hills where we view the remains of a saint, shake our heads sanctimoniously at a tourist wearing a T-shirt with BITCH printed across her bra-less breasts, and take pictures of a pair of bemused-looking ostriches in a dusty pen outside. The following day we visit the island's capital where Milly spots an internet café with a moan of joy. At the market at the water's edge, we buy fruit and vegetables and then walk through the centre of town in search of somewhere to eat, pretending to be more surprised than we really are when we find marble-paved streets and stylish shops and bars.

'What next?' demands Susie, handing me the guidebook every evening, still restless when everyone else is hot and tired and wanting nothing more than iced drinks and the cool beckoning water of the pool. Dutifully, I search its pages, not entirely sure what it is she is expecting me to find.

But after a time the Villa Stamatia grows used to us, and we, in turn, begin to feel more at home there, become accustomed to the momentary blindness of dark, shuttered rooms after the glare of the sun, to marble floors beneath bare feet and the deep silence of mid-afternoon, the siesta hour, and soon even Susie stops trying quite so hard to resist the pace it imposes.

One morning, a few days after our arrival, I step outside and, as usual, reach out a hand to steady myself against the low wall. After a second everything settles and then, after another moment, I understand what, exactly, has changed. The wind, which until now has wound itself around the villa all day long, a constant, vaguely desolate presence, has completely dropped.

That evening, in the taverna down in the village, the owner's wife, a young, heavily pregnant girl, gives up clearing plates and drops down into a chair at the empty table beside ours. She sighs, smiles wearily at us and wafts at the still air with her hand. Milly pushes her food away half-eaten. 'It's too hot to eat,' she says. Her black fringe has separated into tendrils and sweat glistens on her nose and on her cheeks, which seem paler than ever. She had been happier this evening, seeming to grow less sullen in the noisy bustle of the taverna and even responding to our attempts to draw her into conversation. Now her distress seems genuine and we all stop eating and look up at the sky, as if by doing so we will be better able to gauge the truth of her statement.

'It's humid,' says Susie, with a jab of her fork. 'That's the difference. It's going to storm.'

But it does not storm. The air just grows thicker and, as night starts to press down on the mountains that encircle the village, the yachts in the marina sit quite still in the water, not a breath of air disturbing their rigging. The tables in the tavernas along the quayside are filled with families and with groups from the flotillas but the air has a hushed quality now, as if everyone has suddenly sensed that far from being centre stage as they'd imagined themselves to be, they are merely a backdrop for something much bigger. A little group sit out on deck on one of the yachts, playing a game of cards in the circle of light that spreads from a small lantern. In the growing darkness they become more and more distinct until there is something unreal about them, something waxen in the yellowy pool of light, like a tableau or something you have dreamed.

'I vote we do nothing tomorrow,' says Will as we finish eating, looking at poor, pale Milly. 'The children have had enough trekking around for a few days and you and Joe haven't even seen our own little beach yet.' Susie, sitting beside him, is wearing a white dress with thin straps and her shoulders look cool and smooth in the evening light. She appears unaffected by the heat. Will, already tanned and his hair windswept enough for him to be mistaken for a sailor from one of the yachts, has summoned the waiter and he and Susie are making some joke with the young lad as they settle the bill. I think – not for the first time – what a preposterously perfect couple they make and how easy it would be, if you didn't know them, to envy or despise them for their air of easy self-assurance, the aura of wealth and good looks, lightly carried, that emanates from them.

We walk back along the harbour's edge towards the car, Will and Susie in the lead with Milly between them and Samuel nipping backwards and forwards and leaping up into the air, his new boomerang, a bad-tempered concession from Susie, clattering on to the cobbles every minute or so. The water is black now, deep space between the boats, and, as we drive back up the hillside towards the villa, the sky is milky with stars above our heads.

CHAPTER 5

The pathway beneath the villa drops steeply into the olive grove, and then winds down through the trees at a gentler rate. Here, in the first heat of the morning, the cicadas are beginning to stir among the silvery leaves and insects flip and drone among the dry grasses. After a few minutes the light grows bluer, beckoning you ahead, and then, without warning, you are beyond the trees, spat out on to the narrowest of paths with only a stone wall between you and a taut stretch of air, a yawning sky that catches only on the rough edges of the headlands to either side. Below you, in front of you, the wide sea.

Already sweat is running down my back. Everything before my eyes – the sea and the rocks, these cliffs – moves into sharp focus and then starts to warp, threatens to break up completely. I breathe in, greedy for air, knowing that I must find a way to fix this gaping seascape, stop it from imploding around me. I set my eyes upon a small lizard, like a soapstone carving atop the stone wall. It opens an emerald eye at us and then flicks away into a crevice. I shift my gaze to a low, white house on the other side of the bay, focus on its outline. Joe's hand is encircling my arm, holding me steady against the cliff face, but I can hear Milly somewhere above us in the olive grove, her heavy footsteps moving over the rough path, coming up behind us at any minute though she has done her very best to dawdle.

'Let the others go on,' says Joe.

'Milly . . . ' I say, glancing back. But I keep on breathing, in and out, and then the roar starts to recede and I can see Samuel, running along below us now, where the path switches back on itself farther down the hill, and the waves below us are nothing at all, just water moving in and out, beating a lazy rhythm over the shingle beach.

Will registers an absence behind him.

'What's up?' he calls, turning and lifting a hand to shade his eyes. A few yards ahead of him, Susie turns too, mirrors his movement with one hand and places the other on her hip. The blue cotton of her kaftan shivers in the breeze.

'She's fine!' calls Joe. I force myself to step away from the rock face, begin walking down the path again towards Will and Susie, feeling my breathing starting to slow, the fragments of myself loosely cohering again.

'Sorry,' I say as I reach them, my voice unsteady. Only seconds ago I was grateful for Joe's dissembling on my behalf but suddenly his attempt to tidy me away from the scrutiny of others needles me into saying more. 'I'm panicked by open spaces sometimes,' I say loudly, something making me speak before I have really thought about whether I should. 'Stupid really, but it's worse when I come upon them unexpectedly.' The sun is hitting me full in the face. Joe has passed me, is walking on ahead, leaving me to it. Sweat prickles beneath my armpits. For all their triviality, I am shamed by these words. And still I am standing here, exposed on this cliff face like some insect held in the focus of a giant magnifying glass.

'Poor you,' says Susie lightly, but a flicker of curiosity remains in her eyes and already I see that Joe's way is preferable. We make our way slowly down the last stretch of path – Will and Susie on either side of me, as if I am an old person, a child or an invalid – towards the bleached shingle of the little beach where Joe is already lying half-submerged in the water. I have to remind myself that sometimes it is better to skirt around the edges of the truth, or even to lie. Nobody needs to know how this fear of mine is a shape-shifter, pushing its way into every corner of my life, in whatever form it chooses. That trying to conquer it would be as hopeless as the hand of a drowning woman climbing water.

Milly stands apart from everyone else on the narrow length of shingle. The waistband of her denim shorts strains tightly across the width of her back as she bends over to pull off dirty white canvas trainers. Then, with her back to us, she strips off her T-shirt. Beneath it she is wearing a black tankini top, which exposes the roll of her stomach and the yoghurty pallor of her skin. Without a word to anyone, she is off, wading through the water to a slab of rock that slopes into the sea five metres or so away from the shore. Ignoring Susie's call that she should put on some suntan lotion first, she clambers up and sits on the rock, with her chin on her knees, looking out to sea, hardly seeming to notice when her father launches himself into the sea with a shallow running dive and swims right past her, arms ploughing through the surface of the water.

'Coming in?' asks Joe, from his prone position. The invitation is a forgiveness for my indiscretion.

'Maybe later,' I say, signalling an apology.

He clambers out of the water, shedding cold drops of water, and hunts around in our beachbag, throwing out suntan lotion and hats and sunglasses as he goes until he finds the blue-striped plastic carrier bag.

'Ready?' he calls to Samuel, who is a stick-boy in the shallows at the edge of the cove, a silhouette against the glare of the shingle and the hard white surface of the water. Joe holds up one of the diving sets purchased from a mini-market in the village last night and with his other hand he gives Sam a thumbs-up sign. The boy nods in answer, gives a thumbs-up of his own – tentative, unfamiliar to him – and Joe tugs at the moulded plastic that holds the face-mask and snorkel against their cardboard backing.

'He can't swim,' I remind him.

'The guidebook's here if you want it . . . ' says Susie, unpacking the bag that she and Will brought down with them, while I spread towels on the shingle. Behind us is a small beach hut where, Will informs us, sun-loungers and an umbrella are kept. Next time we must remember to bring the key. Susie drops the guidebook on to my towel and then upends the bag, spilling the remaining contents on to her towel. She seizes something and gives a groan of despair. 'And bloody Plutarch, for Christ's sake! That's it!' She examines the book, turning it over as if it is an alien object and then shakes her head. 'Will never manages to bring anything *normal* on holiday.'

'I never got round to him,' I say, looking over with interest.

'You surprise me,' says Susie archly, tossing it to me and then tightening the strings of her bikini beneath the black loop of her hair. 'You're as bad as Will, in your own way. Always hunched up over something obscure.' She lies back on her towel, arranging her limbs, and, a second later, grins to herself. 'Do you remember when that RE teacher confiscated that book of yours? I can't remember what it was but obviously he decided it was absolute *filth*.' She kicks her legs in delight and gives a squawk of laughter. Milly looks back at us from her rock.

'Henry Miller,' I say with a giggle, remembering. '*The Colossus of Maroussi* and not the slightest bit obscene. I don't think Mr Price had a clue, just saw the name and went into a spin . . . ' I think for a minute, add, 'I wasn't terribly discerning though. I read pretty much anything back then – obscure or not – so long as it was set in Greece.'

I glance at Joe and Samuel. They are crouched on a rock in the shallows, examining something they have found. From here they are faceless forms of man and boy, like some kind of cave painting. Will is swimming far out to sea now: the small blob of his head and his two arms, windmilling across the bay, are tiny motions against the blue. Closer to shore, Milly slides off her rock. Already, I see, the sun has caught the tops of her thighs and suddenly I feel sorry for her. There is something about her clumsy progress towards shore – the heaviness of her legs pushing through the water, and the brutality of the mid-morning heat that has turned the skin across her collarbone an angry pink – that makes her seem in need of protection.

'I'm sorry, Milly, but you're going to have to put on some sun lotion,' says Susie, looking up at her daughter.

'I'm going back to the house actually,' says Milly. Then: 'Can I borrow your mobile?'

'Why?'

Milly sighs. 'To ring home, of course.'

'Why would you need to do that?'

Milly lifts her hands to her head and groans as if a great pain has descended upon her in that region. She grits her teeth. 'I need to *speak* to someone.'

'Sorry,' says Susie flatly. 'It costs a fortune to call from here. You'll have to make do with us for a little longer.'

'I noticed there's a phone in the hallway,' I say. 'I don't know if it might cost less to . . . '

Susie shoots a look at me.

'I don't care how much it costs!' Milly cuts angrily across my tentative offering and then immediately looks crestfallen. 'Sorry, I . . . '

'That's enough now!' says Susie, her voice sharpening at her daughter's rudeness.

'Well, I'm going back,' says Milly. She stares at her mother, eyeing her carefully, as if she is weighing up something. 'I would have thought you'd be glad to get rid of me.' Her voice has emptied itself of melodrama, which, conversely, gives her words greater impact. Then she surprises me by moving quickly, darting up the shingle on to the pathway as if scared by her own pronouncement.

'Sorry,' says Susie. She grimaces. 'Again.'

'It's a shame about her hair,' I say, thinking of the auburn curls.

'Oh I can deal with all that,' says Susie. 'She'll come out the other side of it again. It's the lack of charm I find difficult.' She smiles serenely at me, and then wriggles on her bottom down towards the water's edge, where she stretches out her legs in the clear water. I close my eyes, already drowsy in the heat, listening to the little splashes Susie is making with her toes and thinking about the first time I saw Milly, eight months old and no longer the puce, mottled-fleshed humanity Joe and I had seen in photographs, a chubby-legged, grinning creature, entranced by the sunlight on the wall of the bedsit we had just moved into, by the sight of her own pudgy hands.

'Would you watch her for a sec?' Susie had said, scooping up Milly and plonking her on to my lap, going off to visit the bathroom across the corridor before I had a chance to reply, and I remember that I took Milly in my arms, nervous to begin with and then surprised when she appeared to want to stay with me. All I had known of babies until then were bawling grubby-faced infants strapped into push-chairs in town, dummies jammed into their mouths and their noses thick with yellow snot, but Milly had gazed up at me, her dark button eyes taking me in, wriggling around a little, seeking out her father's face for reassurance, but happy to stay where she was for the moment. I remember the robustness of her little body, the surprise of it, and the fine, raggedy cap of down on her scalp, reddish-brown and silky. And I can almost smell the clean, strawberry scent of her, how it rose up to me back then, masking the stink of fried food that used to find its way through the floorboards from the flat below. I open my eyes a little, let my focus drift towards the chatter of Joe and Samuel in the water, think how sometimes it has seemed to me that a baby, new and perfect, might be the only thing that could clear up the mess of me and Joe. Then I sit up straight with a start.

'Joe!' I call. And again, louder this time, getting to my feet. 'Joe!' He and Samuel have waded out too far. All I can see are Samuel's shoulders. From here, his skin looks paper-thin. 'Remember he can't swim!!' Joe raises a hand, half in acknowledgement, half blocking me from view. 'Please be *careful!*' I shout, my voice tight in my chest.

'He's fine,' says Susie who has not moved. Then, in a quiet voice, when I stay standing, watching, 'Joe's quite capable of looking after him, Alice. You know that.' I nod. I should be pleased that Joe is making this effort to befriend Samuel. It is a good sign. 'It won't do Sam any harm,' says Susie. She smiles. 'I sometimes wonder if he's quite with us, you know. He spends far too much time in a huddle over that computer thing of his.'

It is not yet midday, but a thump of heat is already beating from the hills around us, like a pulse, and the towel beneath my body is damp with sweat. Susie loosens her hair from the knot at the back of her neck and shakes it free.

'Shall we swim?'

I follow her through the translucent edges of the water, where tiny fish, their plump little bodies almost as clear as the water, swoop in to investigate my toes. Farther out my feet pass over rougher shingle and then large flat pebbles. Will is swimming in shorewards now, pulling back the water with powerful if unskilled strokes. The water inches up my calves, past my knees and then higher still. A cold current finds my skin. A step farther and the seabed suddenly shelves away.

'Come to join us?' says Susie to her husband as he draws level. She launches out into a breaststroke, giving a little whoop as she hits the water. Right here the water loses the last of its aquamarine tints, its seaside colours. I picture the seabed falling farther and farther away from under my feet, great underwater valleys, dizzying shoals of fish. Before me a deep petrol blue conjures up visions of long voyages and sea monsters around the edges of maps. Endless blackness too, places where the light never finds a way.

'Where's Milly?' asks Will, wiping the water from his eyes and looking towards the beach.

'Gone back to the villa,' calls Susie.

'I'll run up in a minute and see if she's all right.'

'She's fine!' calls Susie, drifting on her back now, her hair fanning out like a black fin behind her. She sees me standing waist-high in the water, still hovering. 'Come *on*, girl!' she bellows in her best games mistress's voice. 'Not afraid of a drop of water, are you?!' Then, treading water for a second: 'Alice, what's the matter with you?' Typically, her wonderment only lasts a second before she flips over on to her front and sets off without me, swimming out towards the rocks, an urgent, bobbing movement across the water.

I think to myself: *I do not know what I am afraid of.* I take a tiny step forward and then another. The current catches at my legs again and as I step forward to steady myself my foot lands on a small, slimy-surfaced rock. In trying to right myself I nearly lose my balance altogether, try to step back and then the sea makes up my mind for me. For the second time today the world skews and then the water is all around me, a great sunlit wash that boils in my ears and nostrils, stinging my eyes and catching in the back of my throat. I come up to the sound of my own coughing and something else besides. Peeling back a dripping curtain of hair from my face, I see Susie, sitting on a rock and gripped by the wild laughter of childhood. Samuel and Joe are looking in my direction.

'Some baptism!' calls Will, grinning from the shoreline.

CHAPTER 6

That afternoon Samuel, clambering over the rocks in the bay, steps straight on to a sea urchin. He thrashes about on a beach towel, eel-like, whilst Will and Susie try to hold his foot still, but they are unable to remove the spines. We return to the villa – Will and Joe half-carrying a sobbing Samuel between them – and then Will and Susie take him into the village in the car, in search of a doctor.

'Where did my mum go?' asks Milly, emerging puffy-faced and pyjamaed from her room, the car engine having succeeded in rousing her from her siesta. 'Oh,' is all she says when I have explained, but instead of returning to her room she sits down at the kitchen table.

'Sorry about earlier,' she says after a minute. She looks down at the table, fiddles with her hair which sleep has parted in various places and which is sticky-looking, in need of a wash. 'Being rude, I mean.'

'It doesn't matter,' I say, smiling at her. 'And you said sorry at the time.' I go to the fridge to check whether we have enough milk for coffee. 'Would you like a drink? Some juice?' She shakes her head but does not move. Milly watches me making coffee, scratching away at a mosquito bite on the back of her arm.

'Why do you like her?' she says suddenly.

'What?'

'My mum.'

I stop what I am doing. Milly's words are nonchalant, a casual enquiry, but she cannot help her hands straying to her hair again.

45

'Well . . . ' I have to hesitate before answering. 'We've been friends for a long time.'

'Yes, but do you think she's . . . ' Milly grimaces, 'a nice person?'

'Of course she is.' But the enquiry has caught me unawares.

'I don't,' says Milly gruffly. 'I don't understand why people like her.' She twists the ends of her hair savagely and I feel a wave of pity for this child in baggy grey pyjamas, lost inside a woman's body right now. Despite her assertions to the contrary, I think she understands precisely what it is about her mother that draws other people.

'It's not always as simple as that, Milly,' I say, wanting to comfort her but not knowing quite how. I think for a moment. 'People like people for different things. All of us are different.' Milly smirks at the cliché.

'So you can understand why other people may dislike her.'

'I didn't mean it that way.' I shake my head, am about to try again when a door opens nearby and I hear Joe's voice calling me. 'People are strange, really,' I begin, without knowing what is coming next, feeling compelled to reach for an explanation before it has even begun to cohere in my own mind. But Milly, hearing Joe coming along the hall-way, has already pushed back her chair, and gone back to her bedroom without another word.

Later, when Susie and Will have returned with a bandaged-footed Samuel – beaming with delight now and making a great show of hopping from place to place – I ask Susie: 'Is Milly OK, do you think?' My tone is light, but just for a moment I think I see a shadow flitting over her expression.

'Why, what has she said?' I notice that she glances across the room towards Will, as if to ascertain whether he has overheard this exchange.

'Nothing,' I say, not wanting to become entangled in the

minutiae of some family dispute. 'Nothing at all. Just that I had the impression . . . she wanted to talk to someone, I suppose.' Samuel lunges on one foot from the other side of the living-room, topples into his mother's lap with a shriek.

'Don't worry,' she says with a little pushing-away motion of her hand, 'I'll see to her.' Then she laughs out loud at Samuel's clowning and I almost believe that I must have imagined the shadow.

*   *   *

From somewhere down in the olive grove I can hear a scops owl, its peculiar electronic hoot carrying on the night air. Beside me, Joe's skin is giving back the heat of the day. I shift away from his warmth but there is no coolness to be found in this bed tonight. I cannot sleep, troubled by Milly's question. I reach for the glass of water beside the bed, drink every drop of it and then lie back again, think about how I might have answered her better, what I might have said if Joe hadn't interrupted us when he did.

CHAPTER 7

On the back seats of buses, on the pier by the river where we go to smoke our first cigarettes, in bedrooms with doors barred against sisters and parents, Susie and I laugh all the time. For me it was laughter made wilder, almost hysterical at times, by an edge of fear. For Susie too? Susie was never easy to read, and it is difficult to decide to what extent her cynical pronouncements were an affectation, a particular strain of modish nihilism. The Yorkshire Ripper is murdering and mutilating women and no one can catch him because he comes down on you silently, from behind, and politicians, pop stars and scientists remind us daily of the threat of nuclear destruction: TV documentaries showing us graphic images of a fate that seems inevitable. Our teachers set us essays with titles like: 'Discuss the Pros and Cons of Nuclear Energy', as if these trite exercises might give us some governance over our future, as if they too were not scared themselves, and then wonder why we can barely contain our contempt for them. We cannot fathom the stupidity of our classmates, blithely continuing with their childish pursuits – girl-guide meetings, ballet lessons – as if none of this is happening, as if an armful of tacked-on badges or a pair of pink-satin *pointe* shoes will somehow make them immune from it all. We think about the imminent nuclear strike all the time. Where we will be when it comes. How we will get home and whether it will be worth trying to save ourselves only to step out into a world where the remains of life fall around us in slow, dissolving drifts like confetti.

A steady job does not seem to steady my mother at all, but

rather the opposite, as if the constraints of her working life – of timetables and paperwork and responsibilities – use up all of her resources, leaving her incapable, or resentful, of order in any other area of her life. My mother says that she likes to operate an open house, a place where we can invite our friends any time we want, but she never understands the rules: the fact that you have to feed people a proper meal when they come and ask what time they'll be getting home again, like other mothers do, and not have strange people with questionable hygiene turning up at the house all the time and staying for weeks on end. There is always someone sitting at the table, rolling cigarettes, eating the last of our food and talking about Cuba or yoga. And so I take to disappearing to the hush of the local library where, among its ordered shelves and footsteps cushioned by carpet, I deal quickly with the demands of schoolwork – most of which seemed facile and pointless – and then move among the shelves, selecting titles on the basis that the authors sound familiar or important, allowing myself to imagine that I could stay here for ever, living the life of the mind which is the only thing that seems to matter to me, when I am here among the quiet hum of the strip lights.

But Susie is more restless than I am, always wanting to be out of the house the minute she can. Simply cannot sit still or even pretend to concentrate in class.

'What's the point?' she'll suddenly snap when reprimanded. She finds none of the comfort in solitude or in books that I do, would be out every night if she could, seeking whatever it is that she seeks. Susie says we should go to parties, to gigs, to nightclubs, to Brighton and to the King's Road in London, a place we have read about in colour supplements and fashion magazines and which, we have come to believe, has transformative qualities, a place where, if we could just find ourselves there, with our feet on that pavement, among *those* kinds of people, we could slip inside another world, leave behind the grey relentlessness of suburbia. We talk our way into nightclubs, dark and smoky, where we should not be, and where we copy the older, more sophisticated girls: the way they dance, with a cigarette held casually in one hand, the way they dress. And we discuss sex all the time: trying to work out how much we understand, wanting to be cool and knowing and for it to come sooner rather than later because until you see what's out there, what you will have to face, you are vulnerable.

Sometimes I feel the need to stand still for a moment, thinking that if I could just gather up everything around me, make all the small pockets of order in my life cohere in some way, I could make them into something bigger and more solid, but Susie isn't waiting for anyone and I am always running behind her, trying to keep up, frightened of missing something.

CHAPTER 8

'What are we doing today?' says Susie one morning, finishing her coffee and putting the cup abruptly down on to its saucer.

'Nothing,' says Milly. 'Please.' We are sitting on the breakfast terrace beneath the shade of the canopy, the first blast of heat of the day already starting to press down upon us. The humidity has kept on rising, day by day, and now the heat has become something frightening, some wilful, damaging force that lies in wait for you, ready to grasp you and shake you in its jaws the instant you step outside the cool rooms of the Villa Stamatia. The maid Alexia – who arrives in her beaten-up car every other day, her two small, olive-eyed little girls in the back – fans herself and says it is the worst heatwave in twenty years. Even at this early hour you can feel it waiting in the hills that surround the villa, know that by mid-morning your limbs will have slowed and by the long hours of afternoon the blood in your brain will thicken until you are almost stupefied by the heat.

'It's too hot to move,' says Milly in a far-away voice, staring out from the breakfast terrace. Where the sea ends and the sky starts is already beginning to blur in the heat and so, for the rest of that day, we sit around the pool, alternating between sunbathing and rolling ourselves through the cool blue water of the pool; all except for Samuel that is for, though the bandage has been removed from his foot now, he has decided that he no longer wants to learn to swim. Joe tries to coax him in but Samuel is adamant and in the end Joe gives up, leaves him sitting in the shade, intent upon the faint tinny rhythms of his games console. Will and Susie sporadically suggest that the other one should remove the toy from him, but it is too hot to argue. In a way I am grateful for Samuel's resolution to remain where he is. I have not been able to persuade Joe of the boy's fragility, cannot make him see that his little stick-like body, those delicate, almost girlish features, could so easily be broken. There, in the cool shade of the umbrella, within sight, within easy reach of all of us, at least Samuel is safe.

*   *   *

Days pass and still the weather does not break. I begin to wonder how long it can go on like this, whether the parched rock of this island might reach a point where it can no longer withstand the sun's ferocity: spontaneously combusts or simply crumbles away into ashes, stirred into the dark ocean by some unknown hand until it disappears beneath the surface. Everyone else complains about the heat, but I find myself strangely excited by what is happening, as if the promise of something alchemical is in the air. I feel as I did when I was a child and the snow falling. Then I would stand at the window for hours, wanting that whiteness to keep on coming from the sky, silently urging it on and on, just to see what would happen in that altered world. Now, as then, I feel as if I am waiting for something.

*   *   *

I am alone with Susie on the sun terrace one morning when she says: 'It used to drive me crazy, you know, you bolting off to Greece with your family every summer.'

'Not every summer,' I say, pushing aside my cup. It is already too hot to drink coffee.

'You were always different when you came back,' she persists. I look at her quizzically. She stares out to sea and then pulls a deliberately sulky face. 'I used to feel that I was missing out on something.' It comes as a surprise to see that beneath the self-mockery uncertainty hovers. 'Of course, it's all very beautiful here, but . . . ' She swirls her hand around in a vague, encompassing motion.

I hesitate before answering. Offering reassurance to Susie feels wholly out of character but it is also a matter of politeness, since it has been clear from the outset that she settled upon this particular holiday with me in mind.

'It was a little wilder than this place,' I say, looking around me at the smoothly painted walls of the Villa Stamatia, its rosebeds, and thinking about the sleek yachts in the village harbour and the holiday homes of wealthy Athenians scattered along the coastline. 'But that was a long time ago.' And I think of the Cycladic Islands, on one of which I happen to have been conceived and where my mother took us year after year when we were young. No more than a rough circle of hot waterless rocks, these islands, with the navy-blue Aegean slapping all around them, all of life pared down to the barest of bones. Scrambling over glaring rocks, turning handstands on bright shingle, my sister Hannah and I would run around half-naked and half-wild all summer long, our bodies burnt brown by the sun. And of Corfu: a tiny stone-cottage on a beach – with pebbles as white and smooth as eggs – lent to us by one of the rag-bag collection of artistic types my mother finds wherever she goes. We travel there in trepidation, made fearful by stories about the ruination of Corfu, but, while there are tourists aplenty to buy jewellery from the little stall my mother sets up in the neighbouring fishing village each evening, what we find is a magical island of dense olive groves twisting over the hillsides, a haunted landscape where the electric buzz of the cicadas somehow finds its way inside the sleep that comes upon us each afternoon, dropping down on our small cottage like an extinction.

'It's all here though, I think,' I mirror Susie's earlier, encompassing gesture. 'It's just hidden beneath the surface a little more. You'd need to get away . . . ' I ponder for a moment, look around me . . . 'up into the mountains perhaps. Or over there.' I point to Ithaka sitting on the horizon, remember what Joe said last night, handing the guidebook back to me: *Just a bare rock with a couple of small villages, Al. That's it.*

'Can't do it, honey,' says Susie with a shudder. 'Remember that school trip to France?'

'The ferry,' I say and then laugh out loud at the memory. 'You almost choking on your own vomit.'

'Rock 'n' roll even then,' says Susie smugly.

An easy silence settles over us for a few minutes. I am just contemplating moving inside, out of the heat, checking where Joe has got to, when Susie speaks again.

'What we need is an adventure,' she announces. Then, seeing that I have not understood, she shakes her head impatiently. 'Oh, any kind of adventure, Alice. One that could go horribly wrong and leave us all in pieces.' I smile at her. 'Don't you miss that Al?' she demands. 'Don't you?' For a moment I am disconcerted by the intensity of her gaze, which wants something from me, is not a dramatic affectation after all. There is the sound of a door opening and closing from somewhere inside and then Susie seems to gather herself in again, her features settling back into serenity. 'I do,' she says, almost to herself.

CHAPTER 9

I am late rising the next day, tell Joe, when he comes to rouse me, that I will follow everyone else down to the beach. When, eventually, I arrive, having made my way slowly but calmly enough down the last steep stretch, I find Will at the back of the beach, fetching an extra sun-lounger from the little beach hut.

'It's getting like the bloody *Tempest* round here,' he complains good-naturedly and before I have the chance to ask him what he means, Susie has come darting across the shingle towards me.

'*There* you are!' She seizes my hand and drags me forwards. 'Where have you *been*?'

'What's the matter?' I say, confused by her demeanour.

'Look!' says Susie pointing. She lets out a giggle. 'Look what Milly found!'

At the far end of the beach, a small boat is bobbing on the waves, just offshore. Milly is standing at the water's edge, kicking at the shingle with her toes and running her hands through her hair in agitation. Beside her, dressed only in a pair of swimming shorts, is the most beautiful boy I have ever seen.

'Where did he come from?'

The boy is kneeling down on the shingle now, anchoring the boat by way of a length of rope, which he is winding around a large rock. Milly stands over him and my own thought is of the shipwrecked Odysseus at the feet of Calypso, but given that the boy's boat is safely moored now and quite clearly undamaged, both Will and I are way off course.

'Who's to say?' says Susie, shrugging. 'I just opened my eyes two minutes ago and there he was, washed up on the beach.' She throws open her arms with deliberate melodrama. 'Milly's kept him cornered ever since, poor creature, so we haven't had time to check his credentials yet. I suppose,' she ponders, 'I really ought to go and introduce myself.' And she is off, flip-flops slapping against her heels and shingle flying as she goes.

Michaelis turns out not to be a mythical figure or even the most minor of Hellenic deities but an American of Greek parentage, 'raised' in California but brought to the island every summer to visit his paternal grandparents. Once, he tells us – squatting down on the sand and addressing us all with that solemn articulacy that seems particular to American youth, born out of a belief that the utterances of any one of their countrymen are sure to be afforded their implicit worth – once, the family had lived inland, but the earthquake of almost fifty years ago wrenched their home and village apart and they were forced to move down towards the coast. Michaelis's grandfather died last year and his grandmother lives alone now, in the long low house across the bay, built with money Michaelis's father earned from a string of restaurants in the States. His parents and younger brother should have been here too, but three days before they were due to fly, Lefteris had been rushed into hospital with suspected appendicitis.

'So mom has to stay behind with him for now,' explains Michaelis, 'and dad came up with a whole bunch of excuses about work and stuff – he can't stand coming back here anyway, says it's too primitive . . . .

'What do *you* think of it?' I ask.

'It's OK,' he replies with an easy shrug. 'I kinda like the primitive aspect of it here. You know, some mornings I get up early, when the sun's rising, and take the boat along the coast to fish and it's just beautiful. I miss having my kid brother around for company, but . . . ' He nods his approval. 'Sure. So long as I have my music and my guitar I guess I can be happy here for a while.' Some kind of strained, joyful noise escapes from Milly. Michaelis looks towards her and then reaches for a book, which is lying face down on the towel beside her sun-reddened thigh. The cover is a glossy black with raised red and silver lettering dripping down it.

'This is yours?' Milly nods vigorously and keeps on going, to exclude even the remotest possibility of doubt. 'I love this guy's stuff!' says Michaelis. 'Did you read his last one?' His voice, I notice, has a slight nasal quality, almost imperceptible to begin with, which, I suspect, might become an irritant after a time, like a small fly perpetually buzzing past your ear.

'Not yet,' manages Milly.

'I'll bring it over for you, if you like. It's awesome.'

Susie, returning from the little shower at the back of the beach where she has been washing the salt from her skin, is just in time to catch these last words. She glances at me with a playful spark in her eye.

'You must come to dinner tonight,' she announces.

'Really?' Michaelis looks genuinely surprised by the offer.

'And bring your grandmother too,' says Susie firmly.

'Oh thanks, but she doesn't speak any English. She doesn't really go out that much either,' he explains.

'Just you then,' says Susie, giving him a dazzling smile.

*   *   *

By seven o' clock that evening, a moussaka, glimmering with dots of deep orange oil that have risen up through its surface or bubbled up at the edges of the earthenware dish, rests in the centre of the table out on the terrace. Alongside it, a bowl of salad and two round loaves of hard-crusted, chewy local bread, like large pebbles smoothed and elongated by the sea. Will has spent two hours in the kitchen, in the hottest part of the day, constructing this moussaka while Joe slept and Susie and I lay full-length on the sofas in the relative cool of the living-room, discussing Michaelis's arrival and teasing Will about how an older woman might be overcome by a sudden predatory urge, a need to defile the clean surface of that kind of beauty.

Michaelis arrives right on time, bearing a bottle of white wine, a basket of bulbous-shaped scarlet tomatoes from his grandmother's garden, a net bag containing a chilled watermelon, and the promised book for Milly. Over wine and dinner and, later, a platter of the chilled watermelon with its damp rind that glistens like bottle-green glass and flesh that dissolves into cold pink grains in your mouth, Michaelis tells us about his grandfather who was hunting in the hills when the earthquake struck and how, just minutes beforehand, he had climbed into a tree to get a better view of the countryside around him and then the force of the quake took hold of that tree and flung him down on to ground, which tried to slide away beneath him when he grasped at it. How, for a few blind, blurring moments, that arid mountainside had a life force of its own, his grandfather waiting for the mouth of the earth to fold itself around him, to swallow him whole.

We question him, wanting to know more about the earthquake, how much of the island was damaged and how long it took to rebuild the capital. Only Susie is silent, unusually so, sitting with her bare feet up on the edge of the terrace and her kaftan pushed up to the tops of her thighs. On another night, her pose might be misconstrued as seductive, an attempt to enact this afternoon's joke for my amusement, but anyone can see that she is only seeking out the little currents of cooler night air that occasionally stir the edges of the solid block of heat that encloses us, up here on the terrace. Besides, notwithstanding the perfect arrangement of his skin and bones, and the deep, liquid brown of his eyes, Michaelis proves himself to be an affable but quite unremarkable boy and Susie has long since given up catching my eye, merely smiles serenely from time to time when he addresses Will or Joe as 'sir'. I watch as she lights another of Joe's cigarettes, the pungent smoke curling up sinuously through the still air and hanging there, like a wavering question mark over her head. Behind her, a family of geckos flickers round the sconced lights on the walls, their exaggeratedly splayed feet like a child's drawing or a cartoon. I follow their skitterings across the wall as they are drawn, one by one, towards the light. It is only then that I notice Milly.

I have paid her little attention during the meal because she has hardly spoken a word all evening, but now I watch her as Michaelis is explaining something about a festival that will take place in the village in a few days' time. She is sitting to one side of him, and has pushed her chair away from the table – where her food remains, half-eaten – so that she is at the very edge of the terrace, beyond the reach of the hot electric lights. She is wearing a black, thin-strapped vest top tonight and the white glare of the moon-light has the effect of stripping away all nuances of colour, so that the curves of her shoulders no longer appear sun-reddened but seem to gleam, statue-like, and her eyes are pools of darkness against the pale glow of her face which looks less rounded and yet, conversely, in the openness of its expression, more childlike, defenceless. And she believes herself hidden, there in the half-light, all wrapped in upon herself as she gazes at Michaelis, as if the movement of the boy's lips, which are just full enough to nod towards sensuality without rendering him effem-inate, are all that matter in this world. But there is some-thing so fierce and wanting emanating from her in this intensely private moment – her mother's bones suddenly visible, there, beneath the softness of youth – that I cannot take my eyes away from her.

Later that evening, after Michaelis has left and Milly and Samuel have gone off to their rooms, Will mixes cocktails out on the terrace and we begin drinking in a hard, determined way because even the stars seem to pulse with heat tonight and there is nothing that you can do about it. It is easier to let alcohol render your body soft and unprotected, to allow the heat inside until it is just an extension of yourself. After a time Will gives up the task of mixing individual cocktails and simply throws a random mixture of everything into a glass jug which he places in the centre of the table for us to help ourselves. Something about Milly's appearance tonight has reminded me not only of her mother, but of myself, as I once was, or perhaps some strange amalgam of the two of us, and I find myself getting deliberately drunk in a way that I have not done in years, since Susie and I were teenagers and falling down in doorways on the way home from parties, or in the early days of Joe and me, when we would hide away from the world, drinking and fucking until our heads were spinning and our limbs were too heavy to move.

Stars are already thickening the sky. Out there on the horizon is the dark hump of Ithaka. In the coming night, I feel its allure again, try – while my words have loosened into a new eloquence and everyone around this table is enclosed by a yellowy bubble of warmth and mutuality – to explain it to the others. I find myself talking about my mother and how, when we were children, she would read to us from *The Iliad* and *The Odyssey:* 'Children's editions, of course, and bits of Greek poetry she'd happened upon. And the myths too . . . trying, I suppose, when we were here amongst it all, to give us some sense . . . ' And how these fragments of a classical education, only clutched at by my mother, had become more than the sum of their parts to me, how their very ephemerality, the random nature of their selection, had somehow enabled them to insinuate themselves into this landscape, to haunt it.

'At least, that's how it seemed to me,' I qualify. 'I'm not sure Hannah ever felt quite the same way.'

'Of course, you know "Ithaka"?' Will asks me.

'What?' Susie says.

'I mean the poem, of course,' says Will. 'By Cavafy.'

'No one knows the poem, Will,' says Susie, after a moment. The small edge of sharpness in her voice finds its way to me and I smile to myself. Will wears his cultural references with a little too much self-consciousness these days, a touch of pedantry adopted in advance of his years.

'I've a copy at home,' says Will, undeterred. 'I'll dig it out for you sometime, Alice, I think it's your kind of thing.' I do not hear Will's next few sentences, too occupied for a moment with the notion of him holding an opinion about me. ' . . . you see, Cavafy says life is what happens *on the way* to Ithaka. That you should never forget Ithaka as you travel towards it but, equally, you shouldn't expect too much of it when you arrive there.'

I frown. 'But then, without Ithaka there would *be* no journey,' I say, leaning across the table towards him to convey the urgency of this thought. 'Nothing would have any meaning. Any . . . resonance.' I glance around me, see that night has fallen quickly. The island across the water is a dark thumbprint on the horizon. 'So it can't help but embody that significance – which is magical, life-giving almost – in some way, can it?'

'Yes, I guess Cavafy knew that too,' admits Will.

Joe is speaking across us now, laughing with Susie about Samuel: how he came to me today, book in hand, wanting to know why the planets don't just drop out of the sky. I fill my glass again and drink. If I carry on like this I will reach a stage I remember well: will see conversation coming at me before it arrives, like a train approaching from a distance, people's mouths moving and their words pushing up against me and then receding, barely processed. But tonight, I am reckless, do not care about such things. Joe glances in my direction and then tails off into nothing, losing his train of thought. I can see, through my own semi-drunkenness, his eyes struggling to focus for a second and then we find one another. The frown line between his eyebrows softens and there is something I remember there, something quick and hopeful. We smile at each other a little, hold each other's gaze as if we were alone. Then Will steps between us, the breadth of him blocking Joe from my sight. He hands another drink back to me, and as he does so my fingers bump against his, overlap. Without looking up at him I hold them there, a second longer than necessary. A present to myself.

CHAPTER 10

'I can't sleep yet,' I say to Joe when, eventually, Susie and Will say their goodnights.

'You're drunk,' says Joe and I laugh, do not deny it, though the truth of it is that my vision has suddenly clarified. Out here, a hot moon hangs in the sky and dark, night sounds are drifting up from the olive grove and I am not ready to shut myself away in the freshly painted air-conditioned rooms of the Villa Stamatia. I am strangely, wildly, awake, as if I, or the air around me, is charged. I take Joe by the arm and he follows me, along the hallway and outside, down the steps and across the driveway. I had thought of the pool-terrace, where the air rising from the sea might bring a little coolness, but now I change my mind, pull Joe towards the path that leads down into the olive groves.

'Where are you taking me?' complains Joe, but he is unresisting.

I lead him onwards, sure-footed, precise in my move-ments, the darkness closing in on all sides until we are out of sight of the villa. Then I pull him to me, kiss him hard, my teeth finding the inside of his lips, and then push him away. 'Take off your clothes and lie down,' I say.

'What here? Are you kidding, Alice?' His words are slurred. He is drunker than I had thought. I smile to myself: I could push him to the ground if I chose to do so.

'Just do it,' I order. I begin pulling off my own clothes now, standing over him, making him wait for me. The moon is yellow and ripe above the blackness of the trees, seems to give a new substantiality to my naked body, and when I kneel down Joe's hips seem slighter than usual between my legs, his body more narrow. I feel as if I could break it at will, an avenging goddess, capable of taking from him anything I choose. Both of us are too numbed by alcohol for real pleasure, but I do not care, push myself down until I hear him exhale, pinning my hands down over his. The blackness of the night presses in on either side of us, the air alive. I begin to move faster and Joe's breath is harsher now, his hands are wrestling with mine, breaking free from where I have pinned them, reaching up to grab at my hips. His body is as familiar to me as my own but the dappling of the leaves turns his face into a mystery – it could belong to him or to another man, to some creature of the woods, a satyr I have chosen to visit myself upon. I can hear his breath coming still faster and again his hands are trying to take control of me, to move my weight in a different way. I pull them away from me, force them down on the stony earth beneath us.

'Alice,' he mutters, wriggling beneath me. Violently, I slam down upon him. 'Alice!' this time more urgently.

'What?' I lift up my arms above my head, rest for a moment, feel the muscles of my stomach stretched and taut.

'Is it safe?' he says. I am off him, so far apart within seconds that it is as if we have never touched.

'Yes!' My voice hisses through the darkness, dangerous and sibilant.

'Shit, sorry . . . I couldn't remember . . . '

I am looking for my clothes. They spill out like ink spots across the ground where Joe is still lying, naked. The white canvas of a solitary shoe glows in the darkness beside his head. Somehow it makes him seem abandoned, foolish.

'Come on, baby,' he cajoles. 'Come back . . . ' I move quickly, not answering, and even as Joe gives up on me, sits up and starts searching for his clothes, I am dressed, shoes in hand, heading back up the path, leaving him scrabbling in the darkness.

'Hold on, Alice,' he calls.

Stumbling up the pathway away from him, I am clumsy now. I bump against low branches, lose my footing, wait for grief to hit me, but some faint mark of the goddess must still be upon me, some lingering trace of potency, for when I think of crying, arms held out before me, feeling my way forward, nothing comes.

CHAPTER 11

Once he has joined me in bed, Joe falls asleep almost immediately. I lie awake, determined to think about what happened tonight, to face up to what it might mean for us, but for some reason my mind will not hold still, keeps wandering away from the subject. After Michaelis had gone, Susie made some flippant remark about him, something about being surprised that he didn't drive a scooter, and then repeated her earlier proposal, about inviting his grandmother to dinner one evening. Milly flared up, reminding her that it was no use, the grandmother didn't speak any English. 'And even if she could,' she'd added, just before she left the room, 'what makes you think she'd want to have dinner with people like us?' The phrase bothers me now, and that tone, as I push the covers back and turn over once again, but I cannot place it in another context. 'People like us'. I shift again. Joe stirs in irritation beside me and I do my best to lie still. It comes to me then.

Our whole class being marched along to the careers room — a little cupboard of a room on the top floor of Daycliffe Manor, with dusty venetian blinds at the small high windows, a few shelves of reference books and catalogues, a card filing system that begins with agriculture and ends with zookeeper, and a pile of local newspapers arranged in fan shapes on a few wooden tables. Here we are left to our own devices for forty minutes, in the hope that we will take the opportunity 'to explore our options'. Once our form teacher has departed, one or two of the more studious girls take down university prospectuses from the shelves and begin flicking through them, but the rest of us treat the experience as an easy distraction from lessons, climbing on the tables to peer out of the high windows or searching for the most outlandish job descriptions they can find in the local newspaper – 'Pig person', 'Christmas elf' – and reading them out loud in earnest, sonorous voices to the rest of the class. Only Susie is horrified by the whole thing, behaves as though she has suffered some kind of moral affront.

'I can't believe they made us do that!' she keeps saying afterwards, running her hands through the spikes of her hair and pacing up and down an empty classroom, her eyes dark with anger. 'How dare they try to pin us down? As if we were still just kids! How dare they try to . . . ' she shakes her head as if she is trying to dislodge something persistent and unwelcome ' . . . to *categorise* us!'

'Don't take it so seriously,' I say, starting to feel uncomfortable about it myself now. Outside the window, the usual lunchtime clamour: shouts of laughter, a tennis ball thwacking against a wall, running footsteps. 'No one else did.'

Susie draws herself up and regards me with cool disappointment. 'They wouldn't, of course,' she says, dismissing the rest of the world with a flick of her hand. 'But *we* should take it seriously, Alice,' she says, blinking fierce mascaraed eyes at me. 'People like us.'

CHAPTER 12

I ignore the mess from last night's drinking, still to be cleared away, and go to the fridge. The shelves are full: feta cheese, swimming in a bath of white, salty water within its plastic wrapping, tubs of sheep's yoghurt, cartons of juice, bottles of beer and of white wine, slices of ham wrapped in soft layers of paper, eggs, a vacuum pack of black olives and two tubs of pale-pink taramasalata. On the bottom shelf sit two raw chickens, each encased in taut plastic film, while in a bowl on top of the fridge are tomatoes, a cucumber, ridged and knobbly, four thick-skinned lemons and a plastic bag full of peaches, all of which Will bought at the supermarket in the little port that lies some miles beyond the village

I drink a glass of water first and then empty the two full ashtrays sitting on the worktop, open the window to cut through the acrid smell that rises up from them, and then hunt for the chopping board. Locating it in the dishwasher, I remove the two chickens from the fridge, drop them down on to the board and then begin tugging at their plastic coverings, tearing each one back in pieces, as though I am opening a birthday present, and then lifting each bird out of its plastic tray. They are narrow-breasted, less plump than a supermarket chicken at home, the skin yellow-tinged and fridge-cold. I carry the first of them across to the sink and run it under the tap. Despite the heat haze outside, the water is icy, makes the bones in my hands ache. I imagine it rising up from some dark source at the island's rocky core. When I have rinsed the surface of the chicken, I turn it and let water run into the cavity.

After a minute, I turn it again, tip the bird neck up and let it drip for a moment. Watery blood runs out of its centre, the last vestiges of life.

'Hi,' says Joe, wandering in. He is wearing the shirt and shorts from last night and his black hair sticks out at odd angles from random, sleep-induced partings. His face is puffy and bad-tempered. He goes to the fridge, pours himself a glass of orange juice and drains it in one go.

'What are you making?' he asks.

'Dinner,' I say grimly, childishly, head down.

'Fine,' he replies, tossing his glass into the sink, not quite hard enough for it to break, and leaving the room.

Already I am beginning to regret starting on this project, wish that I had done it yesterday, or left it till later this morning. There are three knives of varying sizes in the kitchen drawers but now I remember Will preparing the moussaka, saying we really ought to buy some more if we are going to be cooking for ourselves, swearing as he almost sliced into his fingers, blade careering off slippery onion-skin. I take the biggest of the three – though its lack of weight in my hand does not inspire confidence – and begin. For a minute or two I saw away at stretchy, ungiving skin and then give up, throw the knife into the sink and reach for the next.

My mouth is dry again and my hair still feels rough with salt from yesterday's swimming. I shake it away from my face and work on as this first chicken starts to grow warmer in my hands, malleable and slightly sticky to the touch, yet somehow more unmanageable than before. I have done this many times, I remind myself – admittedly with better tools – and I know, am sure I know, where, roughly, bones should end and begin and that here there will be some kind of gap to get between, some leverage to be had, but lack of sleep is making me dull or clumsy because the neat skeletal image I have in my head bears scant relation to the flattened savagery on the chopping board before me, which is fast beginning to resemble road kill. I pause, breathe deeply, stop myself from thinking ludicrous thoughts: that by raising the chicken's temperature in this way, I have restored something of its own will; that it is actually resisting my attempts to dismember its decapitated, stripped body. The heat of the morning finds it way through the window into the cool of the kitchen. I put down the knife. It would be better to shower and dress before I continue any further, clear up the mess of me – and of the dirty ashtrays and half-empty glasses, sticky with the remains of cocktails – instead of adding still more to the sum total of the chaos.

Joe lies on the bed, bare-chested and hands behind his head, and looks as if he is settling down to sleep again. I go to the bathroom, shower and then dress quickly in the lightest clothes I can find.

'I wonder if Michaelis will turn up again today?' I say in a hard, cheery kind of voice.

'Huh?' says Joe, opening his eyes a fraction and then letting them drop. I say nothing for a moment, just busy myself with towels and a beachbag for the day, and then I have to hold on to myself because a wave of rage sweeps over me, a hot, wild energy that makes me want to hurt Joe because no one can be this sleepy so soon after waking and because he is both vulnerable and untouchable, lying there with the bones of his ribcage and the soft skin of his armpits exposed. I slam a drawer shut with deliberate force and Joe opens his eyes and looks at me, a frown starting to form between his eyebrows.

'What's the matter with you?'

The things in my hands fall to the floor, so that I am standing in a soft flurry of towels.

'Doesn't last night bother you at all?' I ask.

'Alice,' Joe says, in a low, warning kind of voice. I focus on the wall opposite me, on the mosquito that Joe smashed against the wall with a book the night before. In the brown mess, I can see a spindly leg skewed outwards.

'You won't even try to change?' My voice is beginning to shake, with emptiness and disappointment. What I want to ask is: do you not love me enough, but I know I cannot say these words without being overwhelmed with first self-pity and then self-loathing.

'I didn't say that.' He is speaking in his quietest voice and in his eyes are fear and hatred, like a cornered animal.

I pick up one of the towels that have fallen at my feet and begin jamming it into my rucksack – which is larger than my beachbag, will hold food and water too if necessary – and then kick off my sandals and take out a pair of canvas trainers from the bottom of the wardrobe.

'I'm going out on my own today,' I announce.

Joe sighs. 'Don't be silly, Al . . .' he says into the pillow.

'I can take a bus somewhere,' I continue, as if he hasn't spoken. 'I might even catch the ferry to Ithaka, seeing as no one else can be bothered to go.' I slam another drawer and Joe gives up on me, makes some kind of indecipherable noise and then pulls a sheet up over him.

'Are you going somewhere?' asks Milly, eyeing my rucksack on the sofa. She is wearing the grey pyjamas and her hair is wet.

'No. Well, maybe just into town to buy some things,' I say quickly. 'I'm not finished in the kitchen yet,' I say, looking away from her towards that room. I do not want to talk to anyone.

'Oh.' Milly's cheeks are still pink and shiny from the heat of the shower. 'Would you do my hair for me?'

She sits in front of me, facing towards the terrace, handing small elastic bands to me at intervals from the packet she holds in her hand. I am dividing her hair into sections and twisting each of those dark sections into tiny plaits all around her head. Her scalp is bone-white and the roots – auburn not black – spring vigorously from it. Something about this situation feels familiar, as if I have been here before. I think of Susie at fourteen, or maybe fifteen: sitting in front of my mother's dressing-table while I backcomb her recently shorn hair into spikes; and then I swap places with her whilst she does the same to mine. Peering at the results of our work out of heavily kohled eyes, we look exactly like two startled hedgehogs.

Milly shows little sign of wanting to converse with me, responding to my admittedly trite enquiries about school and her friends at home with the briefest of replies and volunteering no questions in return. I begin to wonder why she has come to me in this way, why she didn't ask her mother to help, or attempt to do her hair for herself. And yet she seems happy enough as I work my way around her head, plaiting as I go. Sometimes I notice her closing her eyes and smiling to herself, which renders her face softer, momentarily younger than her years, and then her eyes are open again, darting from side to side, following my movements watchfully. When I have finally finished securing all of the little plaits, I smooth my hands across the surface of her hair and just for a second she butts her head against my palms, eyes closed again, like a cat seeking physical comfort. The next moment she is on her feet, gathering the remaining elastic bands together.

'Thanks,' she says abruptly.

CHAPTER 13

When Milly goes to get dressed I load the dishwasher, switch it on and then tackle the chicken again. Knobbly little bones shift beneath the skin as I twist and wrestle with the bird and there is something foetal and grotesque about it that I have to force myself not to notice. By the second chicken, I have abandoned the knives altogether and resort to a bluntish pair of scissors to joint it, shearing my way through skin and flesh, crunching bone and snapping sinew with brutal intent, hoping that the hours of marinating and then roasting will help disguise the mess I am making. After a minute, I manage to split the stubborn bird down the middle and it falls, lopsidedly, into halves. A warm, bloody smell rises up and I see that the bird's liver is still in place, hangs, purple and intact, on the carcass, have to stand back for a second from the quivering dead-aliveness of this thing.

'What the bloody blazes are you up to?' demands Susie, drifting into the kitchen in her kaftan and heading straight for the kettle. 'I need coffee. Fast.'

'I said I'd cook tonight.'

She peers down at the chopping board and pulls a face. 'I don't know how you can face those . . . *corpses* . . . after last night. Will went a bit overboard on the measures, didn't he?' She stretches her arms up above her head and yawns. She is a little pale beneath her tan but otherwise clear-eyed and composed.

'They need marinating,' I reply. 'I should have started them off yesterday.'

'Where's Joe?' she asks after a minute, preparing coffee

while I chop garlic and fetch sprigs of rosemary from the bush growing in a pot on the sun terrace.

'Still in bed,' I say quietly, thinking of the dark shape of him, his deep, untroubled breathing: 'We had a bit of a fight.'

'Oh?'

Straight away I am wondering what it is that has made me tell her this. Soon after I met Joe, Susie and I stopped speaking these kinds of truths out loud to one another. It was a tacit agreement and at the time I had deemed it evidence of a nascent maturity on both our parts.

'Mmm,' I am intent on chopping an extra clove of garlic that I don't really need. 'I want a baby, you see. Joe doesn't.' I smile uncertainly, inviting her to smile back, nod to my rucksack, which is propped up against the table now, a bottle of cold water from the fridge standing next to it. 'I was so pissed off with him I threatened to go walkabout.' But the accusatory quality of Susie's scrutiny does not alter, makes the heat rise beneath my skin. 'Well it's fine for you, you've managed *two* so far– even if you do hate them!' I open my eyes wide, in mock-horror, trying to elicit a response I recognise. I'd expected – wanted – only her usual flippancy, some remark about forcing myself on Joe when he wasn't expecting it, to alleviate my misery.

'What's that got to do with anything?' she flashes, startling me. Her eyes are black with anger.

'Oh look, I was only joking about you hating them . . . ' I say, turning away. The rosemary bruises in my hands, will leave a hot, woody pungency on my fingers.

'For Christ's sake, Alice!' Susie grimaces. 'You can't even walk down that little path to the beach without . . . ' She stubs out a cigarette, half-smoked, in the sink. I stare back at her now.

'That's not quite true . . . '

'And Joe told Will,' she interrupts, 'that you'd barely leave your flat not so long ago. That you're practically scared of your own shadow!' I flinch. Joe's betrayal feels physical, more so since his usual course of action is to pretend that nothing is wrong, even when it is just the two of us.

'You have to get out of fucking Daycliffe,' says Susie, her voice lowered now. 'I can't believe that you're still there after all this time.'

'I'm sorry,' I say, mustering up a polite, reasoned voice from somewhere, 'but I don't follow your argument . . .'

'No?' Susie interrupts again. 'You make me angry, Alice.' Then, dropping into her normal tone: 'I think I'll shower before coffee.' And she is gone, flip-flops slapping lightly across the floor, without another word.

I rub my eyes, blinking back tears, and then strip the rosemary leaves roughly from their twiggy stems and drop them into a shallow dish where a green pond of olive oil, flecked with garlic, is waiting. Though I can hardly breathe, I carry on with what I am doing, throwing quartered lemons into the dish, and last of all the pieces of chicken which I turn in the marinade several times and then arrange in two rows. They sit there, skin side up, beneath the Clingfilm with which I have covered the dish, eight ragged little parcels of life.

*   *   *

I look at the car, parked on the driveway, and think that anyone but me would just get in, drive, that it would take no courage at all. Joe, of course, will be expecting me to make my way down to the beach because this is what was planned last night and because he knows that I, of all people, am no Odysseus, about to launch myself into unknown waters. The thought of this makes me set off at a pace, my rucksack on my back. I am remembering a path I have seen, branching off into the olive groves from the main route down to the beach, a goat-track perhaps, almost indistinct amongst the rough grass and the wild flowers. All the way down through the trees I continue with the charade, convince myself that I am going to take this branch instead of continuing on to the cove as usual, allow myself to imagine that the heart of an explorer beats within me. And when I reach the branch I let myself begin along it, butterflies rising up around me at waist height and the cicadas beginning to buzz in the twisted branches around my head. Then I stop and breathe deeply, hear a goat bleating somewhere nearby, smell something acrid carried on the hot wind. Something moves nearby, a bird perhaps, disturbing the hushed air, and fear catches in my throat because I have made a small, safe world and I do not know how to be alone like this any more. The energy that had me marching down this pathway at full speed drains out of me right there, is replaced by a heaviness in my limbs which is not only the heat but the inevitability of my own nature. *You make me angry, Alice.*

I can hardly admit that I was never going any farther than this, am about to turn back and retrace my footsteps through the flattened grass to the main path without letting myself think about the emptiness that is welling up inside me and will not go away. Then I have a sudden image of what waits for me back there: the Villa Stamatia with its smoothly plastered, perfect surfaces and the manicured borders in the garden; the little cove that lies beneath it, with its calm waters, and the shower we use to wash the dry, burning sea salt from our skins. Then I think of Joe still lying in bed, dozing peacefully because this is what he wanted, what he has decided, and there is something, in my mind's eye, about the set of his jaw, its stubbornness, and the smug, untroubled air around him that makes me want the whole world to upheave itself beneath my feet, for the order of things to be smashed to pieces in great violent blows. And, more than this even: *you're practically scared of your own shadow.*

I breathe deeply. Once, twice, gripping my palms. Everyone is expecting me to be at the beach. They will wonder where I am if they do not find me there, waiting. I turn around, keep on going along that goat-track, down, down into the dark heart of the olive groves.

CHAPTER 14

The house beside the water is long and low and white. An old woman in a black dress and a headscarf is pointing a hose at the small vegetable patch laid out beside it. Tight-skinned aubergines and fat, reddening peppers hang like lanterns amongst the dark foliage and in the courtyard chickens scratch around a long wooden table. I have lost my bearings in the olive groves and it is only when I look back at the shape of the hillside behind me that I realise I have come all the way around the bay and that this must be the house that belongs to Michaelis's grandmother. Not wanting to startle her – she has her back to me and thus may not have noticed me approaching on the path above the house – I call a good-morning to her in Greek, but it seems that she had spotted me after all, for she turns unhurriedly at the sound of my voice, says nothing, but raises a hand and gives an unsmiling nod which has yet a kind of courtliness about it. Then she goes on with her watering.

The path continues past her house and then, almost immediately, it forks. Ahead of me, a small curve of beach, to my left, a path starting to climb through the trees again. Shading my eyes, I see it winding up through the olives and then emerging on barer, scrubbier land high above my head. I stop. I do not want to continue on to the little beach because it feels as if it belongs to the low white house and because there is every chance that Michaelis may appear from somewhere and I do want to have to explain my presence here. But the hillside above me is exposed. There is nothing to grasp at up there, nothing to stop yourself from falling but thin blue sky. I hover, wondering again whether to turn back, but when I glance back over my shoulder I see the old woman has stopped her watering, is shading her eyes and regarding me with curiosity. I take the bottle of water from my rucksack as though this is the reason I have paused, take a long cold drink from it and then, affecting the casual stroll of a weekend rambler, I take the upward path.

I had expected to gain a view of the villa from up here, back across the bay, but it is almost completely screened by a stand of cypress trees, puncturing the blue sky. On either side of me the scalloped coastline of the island falls and rises, even in the far distance the land ending as distinctly as contour lines drawn on a map. I am breathing heavily from the effort of climbing in the heat, my cotton top sticking to my back. A hot wind curls around me. Across the water, Ithaka sits squarely on the horizon, rooted in a blue, careless haze of sea. I stand for a moment, catching my breath, and then, spotting something below me through the trees in the next bay, I keep on going.

This is a wild place I have come to. When you scramble down the hillside, leaving the rough pathway which wants to turn back on itself and take you inland again, you suddenly leave behind the silver, flickering light of olive groves. If you breathe deeply and dare to keep going, you find yourself high above this beach, which is little more than a notch in the cliffs, the land rising up vertiginously on either side of it. Here, just a handful of olive trees cling defiantly to the surface of the earth, contorted and ancient. There is no sign of life on the land below me and, indeed, no immediately obvious way of getting down to it. I consider the distance between here and there: not high enough to cancel any thought of trying, but too far, much too far to jump – and what about getting back up again? Anxiety starts to tighten my chest, my throat.

I crouch down at the edge of the drop. The ground is loose and crumbly here, held together only by long, dry grasses. I see that it would be safer to go down with my body facing towards the little cliff, seeking out hand- and footholds as I go, so I turn around and ease myself over the edge. One handhold gives immediately and I have to clutch blindly at the face of the rock, a shower of gritty earth peppering my face, but I manage to keep a grip, move first one foot and then the next, and though sweat is soon running into my eyes I am more limber than I had imagined myself to be, must have retained some kind of muscle memory from all those hours of gymnastic training as a child, for in less than a minute I have reached a little ledge of rock about halfway down the cliff face. When I step on it with my full weight, it is alarmingly loosely set in the earth. Now I can see that the little ledge of rock is actually an overhang and that there is no possibility of clambering down any farther. My chest tightens, a constriction that moves up into my throat, and I think about climbing back up again. But Joe's words: 'Don't be silly, Al . . . ' And yet if I jump there may be no way back. I shuffle around on that shifting ledge until I am facing the sea, breathe in and out, and then leap.

The electric shrieking of the cicadas is a wall of madness on either side of me, like a door opening on Bedlam. I am on my hands and knees, scrabbling at the shingle. When I am on my feet again I see that the rocks here are like great, pitted bones. Slabs have been heaved up by some force and have slid down again now into this narrow channel of sea, where waves rush into small dark caves and slap into lava holes, boiling at the base of the cliffs. The only evidence of a human presence is a brown plastic beer bottle lying on its side by a tree and a frayed piece of rope by the water's edge. A trail of ants moves across the pebbles beneath my feet and when I look closely I see that one of them is holding another aloft. Putting out their dead. I can see urchins waiting in the pale shallows, little black explosions here and there, and across the water, far out to sea, Ithaka. I think of conger eels: how they like to hide in crevices beneath rocks, and how, if something were to happen to you here, nobody would know, might only come upon your bleached bones many months later. A little sunlit pile of nothingness. And there is something so final and simple about this that I wonder why I have ever allowed myself to be frightened of anything. The heat of the day is throbbing up from the earth. I take a long drink of water, letting it run down my chin, pull off my shorts and T-shirt and slip off my canvas trainers. Then I run across the hot oval pebbles, chart a quick pathway through the clusters of urchins and let myself fall forwards into the cold clear water.

I float like a starfish on my back and later I climb high on the cliff side, grazing my shins on the rough rock as I go. The air is pungent with the warm smell of woody herbs, crushed beneath my feet, and I look out to sea, watch a ferry and then a small flotilla of yachts moving slowly across the vast bowl of the bay. Then I go back down, wipe the blood from my legs and swim again, because you cannot be out of the water for more than ten minutes in this heat without craving another submersion. Afterwards, deciding that nobody is likely to come here except by boat – in which case I would see them approaching long before they reached shore – I take off my bikini.

The small white pebbles near the water's edge mould themselves around your body. Flies land on my legs and on my torso, testing me for signs of life. I flick them away, but after a while it seems to me that it wouldn't matter if you were to die here. That you are already out of time, or part of all time, just by being here. That the sun would still beat down on you and you'd sink into the landscape and hardly know it. I think about my father, whom I have never met because my mother didn't care to stay in touch after my conception, and smile to myself, remembering how, as a teenager, I would write bad, angst-ridden poetry and dream about it somehow finding its way to him, as if tracking him down might make the shifting sands of adolescence solidify beneath my feet. Here, there are no beginnings or endings, or none that matter. I think too about my job, visualise the little office where I let myself in each morning and work almost undisturbed for the whole day, redrafting pages of manuals and then dropping them into someone's pigeon-hole for approval as I leave in the evening, hours passing without the suck of air in the corridor outside as the double swing-doors are opened, without the telephone on the desk beside me ringing, and find that even this little world has come to seem unstable. *Practically scared of your own shadow*.

The droning of the cicadas is soporific, more distant than before. Slipping towards drowsiness I imagine myself as if from above, my nakedness and the fork of my legs, the spill of my breasts. The thought of it pleases me and then the idea of what would happen if someone *were* to find me alone here makes my mind drift farther, into hot, dream-like animal realms. Without opening my eyes, I slide down to the water's edge until I can feel the waves nudging higher and higher, the shock of the cold foam fizzing around my thighs, tightening my skin. The sun is still hot on my hair and my skin, making my blood pulse. I imagine unknown limbs, facelessness, and then I am open beneath the heavens and the ocean all around me, my hands greedy upon myself and the smooth white pebbles bruising my skin, again and again.

Later, beneath the hot midday sun, I slip into sleep and dream of another time.

CHAPTER 15

'We must go to Greece,' my mother said one Easter and so we take a night flight to Athens and then, dry-eyed and mad for sleep on the dockside at Piraeus, board a ferry for Paros, dozing against our rucksacks on the slow-warming deck, above the deep internal thrum of the engine. In Parikia, the main town of Paros, we find cheap rooms and my mother spends her days sketching the curves of the whitewashed archways and of the little churches, eulogising over dinner each evening about the quality of light and how it has a terrible beauty.

'Everything is stripped down to its quintessence,' she explains, when several glasses of Naoussan wine have made her expansive. 'It leaves nowhere to hide.'

She books us tickets for a trip to Delos but Hannah gets food poisoning from a plate of lukewarm meatballs and, after a night of crawling on her hands and knees backwards and forwards to and from the shared bathroom in the corridor, where she hangs over the toilet bowl beneath the harsh glare of the bare light bulb, is now lying in bed, serene in the aftermath but unable to move other than to raise her head for sips of water. I would be happy to stay here with her, reading on the little balcony that juts out over the street below, the shutters pulled to behind me to stop the flies from bothering Hannah, but my mother dismisses this idea.

'Everyone should go there,' she says firmly, pushing a ticket into my hand and steering me towards the door.

*　　*　　*

The breeze gets stronger the moment we leave shore. Within minutes of clearing the inner harbour it is whipping across the deck, surprisingly cold. A smattering of determined sunbathers remain stretched out on their towels, but soon people are pulling on T-shirts again and heading inside the wooden cabin to shelter from the wind. When the seats start to fill up people try going down the steps that lead below deck. I follow them downstairs, where there is more seating and a tiny bar where you can buy Nescafé in polystyrene cups, soft drinks and large bags of potato crisps. I buy a bottle of sweet yellow lemonade and stand alongside a group of middle-aged women dressed in floral sarongs who are discussing the restaurant they ate at last night and the quality of Greek food in general in too-loud voices. Normally I would avoid them but today I half want them to absorb me into their midst, suddenly conscious, in this over-intimate space, that I seem to be the only person travelling alone on this boat.

But all the summer-bright clothes on board are not enough to ward off the weather. As soon as we clear land the full force of the wind hits us and the little boat immediately begins to pitch. As the first wave smacks against the side of the boat, people grab the backrests of the bench in front of them and smile or raise their eyebrows at one another.

'Whoooo!' says someone cheerily. When the second wave hits, everyone grins less certainly.

'It'll settle down once we're out to sea,' one of the floral women assures the others, but she is wrong because everything soon gets worse, the little boat starting to heel over alarmingly, first one way and then another. The boy serving behind the bar is summoned up on deck by a guttural shout from above and everyone's eyes flicker, watching him go, trying to gauge what might have been said to him.

'What's going on?' says a mother, holding tightly to her young baby.

Minutes pass and soon people have stopped talking, are clinging on to anything solid, bracing themselves for the next wave. Then a young German man sitting adjacent to me, his body determinedly immobile, suddenly shudders and a horrified moan escapes from him. The next moment he is clapping a hand to his mouth and making a dash towards the steps.

'Shouldn't they be turning back if it's this bad?' wonders an elderly woman in shorts and walking boots, who is sitting on a bench in front of me. Her husband says nothing, just presses his fingers into his forehead to contain something, and stares down at the deck. One by one, as the waves catch at us, throwing the little boat forwards, sideways, other passengers follow the young German, staggering across the lurching floor like drunkards

A young girl in the corner clutches her boyfriend's arm and begins, quietly, to cry. The boyfriend bends over her, presumably reassuring her though you can hardly hear a thing over the slamming of the waves against the flanks of the boat and the whinnying of the engine.

'Come on,' orders the spokeswoman for the floral brigade, suddenly moving. She heaves a straw shopper up over her shoulder and across one of her heavy breasts. Where the straps of her swimming costume bite into her back, the skin bulges in protest, biscuit-brown, shiny with sun-oil and blotched with spreading freckles.

'Up on deck,' she orders. Then she looks at me. 'You're better off in the fresh air, love. And we'll have a lot more chance if this thing goes over.' I nod and watch her and her companions holding on to one another for safety as they cross the cabin, broad buttocks and shivering thighs disappearing up the steep steps. The smell of engine oil is inside my nostrils, catching in the back of my throat, and the noise of the engine, fighting against the waves, has found its way inside my bones, is throbbing within my skull. I wait a few minutes and then make my way around the edge of the cabin towards the steps, trying to appear nonchalant and praying that I am not going to be sick.

The floral woman was right about one thing: the wind whipping across the narrow deck sweeps away any thoughts of sickness. I steady myself as best I can and edge my way across the boat, finding myself a spot well away from where that group have settled themselves, halfway between the prow of the boat and a tiny life raft. I drop down to a crouch and wedge my rucksack into a corner and then I lie down, almost flat, with my head propped up against the rucksack and watch as the deck rears up in front of me, pushing up into the sky. After a while, I begin to discern a rhythm, know that the moment when we seem to hang in mid-air is always followed by a slam and the flying of spray and groans rising up all around me as the ocean sucks us downwards again. It is surprisingly warm here, lying against the sunny deck in this sheltered spot, my rucksack cushioning my body. I watch the captain – an old man in faded blue trousers, with a barrel chest and muscles in his thick brown arms like cables. His voice booms out from that barrelled chest, rich and guttural, issuing orders to his crew, and then he is laughing about something – the poor, white-faced passengers perhaps, who cling to the sides of his boat – and his wide brown feet, bare of shoes, move surely across the juddering deck, his body untroubled by the chaos of the ocean, and suddenly you know, without a doubt, that there is nothing he does not understand about this sea that boils and hisses like a blue cauldron all around us.

I find myself thirsty again but I do not want to go back inside so I take from the side-pocket of my rucksack the peach that I bought from a stall near the quayside and which I have managed not to squash by leaning against it. A man sitting a few feet away from me fixes his eyes on me and then on the peach as though it represents a betrayal, or an atrocity of some description, and then in an instant he has his back to me, is hanging over the edge of the boat, his ribcage heaving. A young crew member, who looks more North African than Greek, his features sharp and his skin almost burnt black by the sun, catches my eye as he passes, grins and clutches at his throat dramatically. I grin right back at him, lift the peach to my mouth and take a huge bite. Juice runs down my chin, over the furred skin of the fruit on to the deck. The flesh of the peach is warm and honeyed in my mouth and I lie back, moulding myself to the deck of this little boat that will not be deterred from nosing its way forward through the maddened blue sea, watching along the length of my body as my feet rise and then dip with the motion of the boat and, as the shore disappears behind the horizon and we are alone, cupped here between the dome of the sky and the frantic ocean, everything begins to fall away from me: these other passengers locked in by their sickness and distress, my mother and Hannah in that airless little room within the maze of Parikia's streets, the hours in class, trying to confine everything between neat, ruled lines, even Susie, back home in England. Out here on deck, I am an adventurer, not cowed by my aloneness but, in this moment, defined by it, made more by it. Everything falls away from me and I am here in the sun with the rough, pitted stone of a peach in my hand, shreds of bright orangey-yellow flesh still clinging to it, and I am the happiest I have known.

*   *   *

In the harbour at Delos, everyone hovers around the boat, taking tentative steps and testing their legs like old people, or staring down intently at the hard-baked earth beneath their feet with a kind of hungry reverence. Impatient with them all, I set out on my own. The sun beats down upon my shoulders, exposed by the narrow straps of my vest top. It is flaying heat, reminds me of what my mother says about everything here being stripped away, but my shadow stretches tall across the stones beneath my feet and the new spirit of solitude is rising in me again. 'This is my true self,' I say in wonder, under my breath, as I pass along the

Terrace of Lions – the spare, elegant lines of their bodies frozen, attentive, caught in some collective registering of a frequency beyond the range of the human ear, sightless stone eyes staring impassively at history – and because I am young and entirely alone here these words seem to carry a profundity, do not seem as self-regarding or earnest as they ought. Lizards skitter across mosaic floors and around the bases of broken columns. All around me a constant hot wind combs the dry grasses of this island and it is because I am alone and my body is fully awake, as strong as Artemis the huntress whose birthplace this is, as attentive as the Lions, that it comes to me: a numinous whispering, pushing against my ears until it is all I can hear.

Back on board the boat, the wind has dropped and voices rise up all around me, high with relief. We could be anywhere or nowhere, with crisps and cokes being consumed and the flat, prosaic sea an incidental backdrop. In Parikia, I find my sister sitting on the balcony, sipping water and the colour beginning to return to her face. She and my mother listen to the story of my voyage with interest but they look towards the harbour, out across the streets of Parikia – which turn in upon themselves like the whorls of a shell and where the afternoon is a thick blanket of heat – with only the semblance of belief, because when you are in a safe place it is hard to believe that anywhere else exists.

CHAPTER 16

Back at the villa, Susie draws me into the privacy of her own room, which is cool and shuttered against the late-morning heat.

'I'm sorry I was so brutal,' she says, facing me.

'That's OK,'

'Will and I had had a bit of fight too – squabbling about Milly.' She lifts her hands to her head. 'And with a hang-over to boot . . . '

'It doesn't matter. I went for a walk, to think about things.' I sit down on the edge of the bed, facing away from her. I wonder if I could even begin to explain what is wrong with Joe and me.

'I can't believe you just ran off like that!' says Susie. 'You might have taken me with you.' She says nothing for a minute and then I feel the bed give under her weight, as she sits down on the opposite side from me. 'Do you remember the first time, Al?'

'What?' I ask, looking round at her, not understanding.

'When we ran away.'

'Oh *that*,' I say and then I laugh, the tension leaving my body as I recall a morning in winter, long ago, when Susie was quieter than usual on the way to school.

'I'm going to London,' she'd said. 'Are you coming or not?' A casual kind of announcement, which I hardly took seriously until she turned in the opposite direction, towards the station. And then the two of us standing in silence on the platform, a cold wind sweeping in from the grey river in the distance, carrying spiteful slaps of rain, and me not asking anything because there was still time for this mood to pass and for us to slip into school before assembly.

'I don't think I really believed we were going to do it until we were on that train,' I say, remembering how we'd stood and argued when the train pulled into the station and everyone else was getting on or off, and then Susie, seeing that it was starting to leave, giving up on me, setting off at a run along the platform until she drew parallel with one of the doors, her hand reaching out for the handle. A picture comes into my mind: her thin wrist – fragile within the thick woollen cuff of her school coat – against the grey air and how she'd wrenched at the moving door and it had opened, swinging out dangerously, a heavy metal wing which could flap just once against your bones and smash them to pieces.

'Oy! Get away from there!' yelled the ticket collector, jumping out of his little kiosk and blowing his whistle over and over again, but Susie already had a foot up on that moving step, seemed to hang there for a second above the gap between the train and the track below, where the dark chaos of turning metal and electricity waits, and then, somehow, that door was slamming shut behind her.

Susie settles herself back on the bed, first thumping air into a pillow for her head to rest on. 'Well, *you* were lucky to make it at all, Al. You were nearly left behind.'

I frown, trying to remember the details. 'I think the train must have slowed down for a minute, because of all that whistle-blowing . . . ' I say.

The gesticulations of that ticket-collector, like a puppet in the distance. Another door passing me and the cold metal handle finding its way into my hand and me pulling down on it, dragging it towards me with all my might and then propelling myself forwards into a space that seemed to hang in front of me, a blur of confused light that could not be trusted to catch me. I found myself on my hands and knees, the burnt, rubbery smell of the floor of the train filling my nostrils, at the feet of a man who was standing in this outer part of the carriage, smoking a cigarette.

'What the fuck . . . ?' he'd said, but he managed to lean out over the top of me and pull the door closed. I'd scrambled to my feet and gabbled something that was both apology and thanks. The train swerved and clattered and I fell forwards down the corridor, beside the first-class carriages where businessmen were sealed in bright air behind sliding doors, straight into Susie. We'd collapsed against one another, celebrated our survival with wild, triumphant laughter.

Here in this whitewashed room with Susie, I can recall little of the physical facts of the journey, have only a vague sense of its general griminess and of hot air scalding the backs of my legs from the heaters beneath the seats, but I can still feel the elation, the knot of excitement in my stomach hardening as we left Daycliffe behind, because I did not know where that day was going, never imagined, when I'd woken that morning, that anything other than the slow ticking clock of the school day, the familiar pattern of those hours, might be waiting for me. It was as if we had slipped our skins, were ghostly shapes of ourselves, hardly existing here among the real lives of other people. Susie had said little, just slouched nonchalantly in her seat, gazing out of the window, and I had not wanted to ask her any more in case with clumsy words I broke the delicate unspoken gift of the day.

'But I wonder what we thought would happen?' I say, lying back on the cool sheets beside Susie now. She is stretched out, with her hands beneath her head, staring up at the ceiling. 'It's not as though we *did* anything when we got there.'

'We went to see the Queen,' she corrects me and the two of us giggle like children, recalling how at Victoria Station we'd stood in front of a tube map, with too many people craning around us, jabbing at various points on the map with their fingers. I remind her how we'd known that the

King's Road was in Chelsea but that there was nowhere on that map that seemed to correspond with this, how in the end we'd left the station and just started walking, followed the signs for Buckingham Palace because, we'd agreed at the time, that would be a central sort of place to go. When, finally, we saw its boundary walls on the other side of the road we began to joke about things, feeling surer of ourselves, just because we'd managed to navigate our way somewhere. There were groups of Japanese tourists with cameras, and everyone staring through the railings towards the palace, waiting for something to happen. But the rain kept on falling that morning, in soft, almost invisible sheets, and though a small black car drove in through the gates and beneath an archway, there was no movement at any of those blank-faced windows.

'Don't forget that delightful picnic in the park,' I remind Susie, thinking of the stale sandwiches we'd bought from a newsagent's and how we'd sat in Green Park, on the edge of a damp bench, feeding the remains of the bread to the pigeons. 'And the sightseeing,' Wandering along Piccadilly without knowing where we were going or why, beneath the archways of the Ritz, past airline offices, tourist boards and bookshops, and in the fading light of the afternoon, the scruffy neon of Leicester Square already drawing people in. I remember that there were voluble hordes of foreign teenagers everywhere, gathering around theatre kiosks and cinemas. I can still feel their exuberance: how it surrounded them like a warm, generous, brightly lit bubble and how they spilled out over the pavements towards us or walked backwards into us with their cameras aloft, as though they would have been happy to share their good fortune and high spirits with us, would have liked to enclose us in their pool of light. But there was something immovably apart about the two of us, some growing, childlike desolation about our dark school coats and damp, rain-soaked shoes.

'We should go home now,' Susie had said eventually,

without looking at me, and I could not tell whether she was disappointed – in herself, or me – or not.

'Well, at least we went,' says Susie now. She grins, wrapping her arms around herself, and then rolls over on to her stomach, her head turned towards me, eyes widening in mock-alarm: 'Do you remember how it all kicked off when we got back?'

'No, I can't.'

'You must!'

'No. What happened?'

'Being marched along to the office?'

'God, I'd totally forgotten that bit!' One of the school secretaries had spotted us boarding the train that day. Just before we'd entered the headmistress's office Susie had signalled silence to me and, once inside, she'd begun to weave some story about a boyfriend pressuring her to sleep with him; the confusion of it all; needing time away from everything to think. And, she'd added – remembering me halfway through this performance – someone to confide in. I recollect thinking at the time that surely, just by looking at the pair of us – with our school skirts tacked up to thigh level and our kohl-bruised eyes – you could see the lie of it, could hardly believe anyone could be fooled by such a tale of innocence, but Susie was proved right that day because her story actually brought a moderating of punishment – even a modicum of sympathy – our way, both of which made us double over, clutching our hearts with silent laughter in the corridor outside.

Will's voice echoes suddenly in the hallway, calling for us.

'I suppose we'd better go,' says Susie, getting up from the bed with reluctance. 'We've been missing for ages.' She slips her feet into her flip-flops and draws her hair back over her shoulders. 'You look like some kind of outback creature,' she reassures me as I check my wild and sunburnt appearance in her mirror. 'You know the reason I was such a bitch this morning?' she says quickly, in a lowered voice, as the footsteps outside come nearer, begin closing down upon us. 'Will is *desperate* for another child. So at the moment the very mention of babies . . . ' She does not finish the sentence because Will is at the door, is about to open it, but the look on her face, as if she is being forced to look at something utterly repellent, tells me all I need to know.

CHAPTER 17

Michaelis arrives at the beach in his boat the next morning to say that he is going fishing – does anyone want to come along? Milly grabbed a T-shirt the minute she heard the thrum of the outboard motor across the bay. She has, I notice, made a conscious effort to sunbathe this morning instead of cramming herself as tightly as possible beneath the shade of an umbrella and complaining at intervals about the heat. Now she distracts herself from Michaelis's presence by rubbing suntan lotion on to her legs with a vigorous punishing motion, as if kneading her body into some other form.

Will says Samuel may go so long as he wears the life jacket Michaelis has thought to bring with him, and on the condition that Milly goes too. They are not to leave the bay itself, though, he warns. Milly says nothing, even trying to enact disinclination as she is getting her things, while Samuel, who has persuaded Joe to carry him out on his back – is already slithering over the side of the boat.

'Hurry up,' he crows exultantly and his sister follows him into the water, carrying a towel in front of her.

The sky above Milly's head is high and endlessly blue today. You could fall into it and never surface. She is trying very hard not to hurry, and suddenly I feel her exposure, all eyes upon her and she alone out there, the violent morning sun beating down on her tender, already-pinkening skin. She picks her way across the shifting sands of the sea bed, the water dragging against her legs, and Michaelis is waiting, feet planted casually on the solid boards of his boat, watching, and all of us here on the beach, smugly contained by our adulthood, are also observing her progress. I notice that she has forgotten to take her sunglasses with her, is squinting into the fierce, reflecting light, feeling her way forward almost blindly. When she reaches the boat she tries to follow Samuel's example by pulling herself up and trying to throw one leg over the side, but the boat has drifted a little farther from shore now and Milly, besides having no adult to assist her, is less agile than her brother. Waves caused by the ferry to Ithaka, which has just passed across the mouth of the bay, are making the boat buck in the water, impeding her attempts still further. I look for Joe, but he has swum out to the rocks and is too far away to notice the trouble she is having.

'She's can't manage on her own,' says Will tensely, getting to his feet.

'I don't think she's strong enough,' says Susie.

And I would like to sweep us all away from this beach, leave Milly here alone, unjudged. Will holds back because Michaelis is bending over now, his arm, brown skinned and lightly muscled, reaching out to help her. This time, on her second attempt, Milly manages to launch one thigh over the gunwale, where it gleams for a moment, heavy and pallid in the harsh sunlight, like some strange anaemic creature pulled up from the sightless depths of the ocean, and then, with a great heave and a wave to assist her ascent, she manages an ungainly roll into the boat. She disappears from sight for a second and then she is scrambling to her feet and as the boat tips at an alarming angle Michaelis is grabbing her again, pushing her down next to Samuel. When she is finally seated, he gives a wave and a grin to the audience on shore and then tugs expertly at the outboard motor's ripcord. A moment later the engine chokes into life and the boat zips away towards the other side of the bay, the faint smell of petrol drifting back to shore and white water foaming in the wake of the boat like a wedding train. Eventually the air empties of the sound of the motor and they are just three figures being drawn out to sea. In a way I am glad to see them gone and yet without them our little beach seems empty, somehow less satisfactory than before.

*   *   *

Just before lunchtime Michaelis, Milly and Samuel return with a plastic bucket full of small, silvery fish. Michaelis says they are for us, but we have planned to eat in the village this evening and insist he should take them with him. He tells us that they were his grandfather's favourite, that his grandmother will prepare them as she always did for him, scaling and gutting them before frying them whole in olive oil for dinner. Later that evening, Milly, looking out from the terrace towards where the low white house lies, swears she can smell the aroma of frying fish drifting on the warm air across the bay.

*   *   *

And so it is that Michaelis starts to become drawn into the life of the Villa Stamatia, arriving most mornings in his boat or walking around the bay to join us for dinner in the evening. From the little rocks close to shore, he and Milly dive for coloured shells, Michaelis teaching her how to reach the bottom by blowing the air from her mouth, so that all we see from the beach are upended legs against the sky and streams of bubbles breaking the surface, until Milly emerges triumphant, arm aloft and black hair plastered against her face. Joe shakes off his torpor and fetches the snorkelling equipment from the villa and before long there is a whole party of people in the water, all of them taking it in turns to snorkel and spot fish and, despite the bruising heat of midday, our little bay is the most animated it has been since our arrival.

I join them for a while but then go back to shore to keep

Samuel company, since he is still refusing to set foot in the water no matter how much he is teased or cajoled.

'Leave him alone!' I tell Joe when he pretends to consider dragging him in and this seems to set me apart as trustworthy in Samuel's mind, for he sits down beside me on the sand and rewards me with half an hour's description of some little science experiment he's planning to set up the minute he gets home. I listen carefully and try to ask the right questions at the appropriate moments until he decides we've exhausted the subject.

'I think I'm going to read my book now,' he informs me kindly, clearly mindful of my feelings, and as he takes himself off into the shade, I can't help smiling at that particular mixture of earnestness and enthusiasm which, in an oblique way, reminds me of Joe when he'd just begun teaching and was still boyishly evangelical about it.

Every day, before Michaelis arrives, Milly seeks me out, finding me on the breakfast terrace or waiting until we are all on the beach before approaching me and asking me to plait her hair for her, to thread the beads she bought in the village over the ends.

'You could ask your mum to do this for you, you know,' I suggest one morning when we are sitting on the rocks a little distance away from the rest of the party. 'Not that I mind,' I say hurriedly, seeing Milly's expression.

'You're gentler,' she says. 'And anyway, she wouldn't want to.'

And it's while I am plaiting her hair that I begin to tell her about her mother and me – when we were younger.

CHAPTER 18

Our form teacher, a spare-featured woman with a clipped accent and a reputation for brooking no nonsense, tells us that this, our GCSE year, is one of the most important of our lives and that we must all expect to work harder than ever.

'I'd expect you all to have a good idea of what you want to do with your future by now,' she says. 'And I do mean *all* of you,' she barks, giving a sudden sharp rap on the desk with her ruler so that those of us who are slouched over our desks doodling on notebooks, or fiddling with pencil cases or bags, shoot upright in our chairs. But Susie, staring determinedly out of the window and humming under her breath, might just as well have her fingers in her ears.

The two of us have made ourselves so unapproachable by this stage in our school careers that no teacher ever exhibits signs of wanting to discuss our futures with us on a personal basis. On the one occasion I try to raise the subject with my mother, she says, 'I'm sure it will all fall into place, darling,' and leaves it at that.

'Alice is extremely able, but she seems unhappy,' said one of my reports from that year. Which, I see now, and probably suspected then, meant that they did not know what to do with me, that they found me more puzzling and troublesome even than Susie who, as a persistent run-away, was at least easy to classify.

In the beginning, she would disappear only for a morning or an afternoon. If I happen to be there at the precise moment the urge seizes her, she takes me along: into town, where we wander around the shopping mall and talk to the boys on their way to the dole office, dodging into shops to hide from friends of our mothers; or to the river where we sit on the broken pier, smoking cigarettes and kicking at the damp, rotting wood, the bolts that bleed orange rust. After one particular absence, our form teacher keeps me behind longer than she does Susie in order to point out the danger of being easily led. It is a weakness in my character, she says, against which I need to guard, and I just stand there and say nothing, grow even more sullen, because there is no point in telling her that I am at my strongest when I am with Susie, that anyone with any sense could see that danger lies everywhere in this place but with her.

But as the year passes, I start to work harder than before. Though I have no real sense of what lies beyond, the definable certainties of exams and study notes hold an appeal for me, begin to seem like a solid ladder with easily achieved rungs which, if I could just climb it successfully, might transport me . . . somewhere. It is then that Susie starts to take off on her own.

She disappears for a whole night, and then, soon after that, two or three nights at a time, sometimes more, before arriving back at school with a look on her face that means nobody better ask her any questions. The first few times she fails to return home, her parents are frantic. They call the police and close the pub for the evening, drive up and down the streets of Daycliffe searching for her, but pretty soon the police refuse to take them seriously because Susie leaves notes saying that she will be back soon, and she is, after all, nearly sixteen years old. Her parents start to despair of her because no matter what punishments are meted out to her at home or at school, it is only a matter of time before they find another note pinned to the notice-board in their kitchen.

At first I pester and pester Susie, desperate to know where she has been, wanting and not wanting to be out there with her when she slides away into the darkness, but she tells me so little, sometimes mentioning the name of somebody we might have met at a party or in one of the cramped back rooms of smoky pubs where we go to watch bands play, saying she drank too much or smoked some dope and crashed on this person's floor for the night. These are people who barely seem to notice me standing beside Susie's cool beauty, who turn their backs to me when they are talking to her as if to ease her away from me, so after a while I make myself stop pushing Susie for information – about how you can drop yourself into someone else's life for a day or two and then pop up out of it again just as suddenly, like a jack-in-the-box – in case one of these quick violent friendships of hers which flare up so quickly should fail to burn itself out as usual. I comfort myself with the fact that there will be time for Susie once the school year is finished.

But even Susie is forced to think about the future because her father is losing patience with her, says she's not sitting around at home this summer and that she'd better find herself a job or come to help in the pub kitchen if she can't think what else she wants to do. After a few weeks and without any apparent enthusiasm, Susie mentions that she has applied to study fashion at the art college where my mother works. She has taken to making her own clothes – oddly shaped garments that don't seem to work until she has put them on – and, she says, she only needs to pass four exams to be accepted. When I question her about the course, she brushes off my enquiries, speaks in vague terms about having interesting people around her, but all the time she talks about this future of hers as though it belongs to someone else.

And then one day, just before our exams are about to begin, Susie turns up at my door with a sports bag over her shoulder.

'Let's go,' she says.

'Where did you get that from?' I ask, eyeing the bag.

'It's my dad's. It's the biggest I could find.'

'Where are we going?' I ask.

'Anywhere,' and she starts up the stairs.

I follow her up to my bedroom but I am suspicious of that bag.

'Why do you need a bag that size?' I question. 'Where are we going?'

'Oh for Christ's sake, Alice,' she snaps, swinging round to me and dropping the sports bag at her feet where it lands with a thud. 'Stop going on about the fucking bag, will you? It's just not important.'

I narrow my eyes at her, fix her with what I hope is a penetrating stare, which she holds for a moment.

She grimaces. 'Anywhere,' she says quietly. 'Anywhere but here.'

'For how long?' I persist.

'How should I know?' she fires at me, throwing her hands up in the air and marching over to the window. 'Maybe for good.' She stares out at the backs of the terraces that enclose us.

'Oh look, I can't, Suse,' I say. 'Not right now. Not when we've got exams coming up.'

'Exams?' She stares at me in disbelief.

'Yes,' I say as firmly as I can.

She does not move for a full minute, just keeps on staring out of the window. Then: 'Fine.' She reaches down for her bag and heaves it up over her shoulder.

'Come on, Suse . . . ' I say, but she pushes past me, is thumping down the stairs and out of the door before I can stop her. I fully expect her to be absent from school the following morning but when I arrive she is seated at her desk. For the rest of the day she will barely speak to me, merely regards me with a sorrowful look every time I try to explain.

All through the long, empty afternoons of May and June I sit in a stifling classroom, with the scratching of pens and the rustling of papers all around me, the thud of tennis balls on the hard courts beneath the window and the shouts of girls on the athletics field ringing through the clear summer air, completing paper after paper until the bones in my right hand begin to ache.

'Why are you bothering,' says Susie, 'when you know you'll pass anyway?' And I cannot tell her why, know only that if I stop now, let go of this, it would be like falling through thin air. And I would never dare to tell her that I have started to see something circuitous, futile even, about the route *she* is taking: no matter how hard she strikes out, it always seems to bring her back to where she started. It is not exactly that I have lost faith in her, but that there is an urgency to complete this thing of my own which makes me want to put Susie away for the time being, at least until the exams are finished. Then, I feel sure, everything will be easy again. But as soon as she has sat her chosen papers, Susie disappears again, not bothering to come into school for the remaining exams she is due to sit. Her father, meeting my mother in the High Street, tells her that they no longer know what to do about this wayward daughter of theirs. She turns up again briefly, just as the main body of the exams is finishing, and we talk about what we might do for the summer, some loose notion of buying a tent and taking it to France, but then, just a few days later, Susie telephones me to say that her grandmother in Ireland has fallen ill.

'Mum says we have to go to Dublin for the summer,' she explains.

If she had shown the slightest disinclination to go, I would have seized upon it, sick grandmother or no, but she is puzzlingly compliant, appears already to have forgotten the plans we had made and actually seems cheered by the prospect of a summer hundreds of miles away. And so, as the evenings lengthen and our final year at school together draws to a close, I see that I have left it too late and that Susie is slipping away from me for good.

CHAPTER 19

'Shouldn't you be keeping cool at this time of day?' I look up to see Will standing over me, almost silhouetted by the glare of the sun. He squats down beside me and before I have a chance to make any sense of it, he is reaching out his hand. A throb of panic jars me and I am pushing myself up on to my elbows – one hand preparing to block his approach – when his fingers reach me. He presses lightly against my collarbone. 'You're going to burn across here if you're not careful.' He looks past me, farther up the beach. 'You too, Suse, it's hotter than ever today.'

'Don't fuss,' says Susie, lazily. She stretches out an arm, however, and examines her skin, which is a pale golden colour, the darkest it will ever go. A piercing shriek from Milly grabs everyone's attention. There is a great flurry of splashing and Milly's strong calves are pounding through the water towards us, Michaelis chasing behind her. Small wavelets fizz up around her legs and the firm white flesh on her thighs and torso shivers as she sprints in our direction. Then she is before us in the shallows, her swimming costume rising up over her buttocks as she bends, lifting water in her hands as though to wash herself, like a figure in a painting, but instead tossing it into the air in a great arc and then flailing at the surface of the sea to fend off her pursuer. Michaelis yelps and retreats into deeper water, Milly running to catch up with him, and there is something magnificent and liberated about her strong white form, a statue breaking out of the shape it has been holding.

I turn to smile at Susie but see that her face is virtually

expressionless, except for an air of watchful repose, as if she were on guard for any possible incursions, like the lizards who inhabit the cracks in the walls around the Villa Stamatia and who venture out to sit, motionless, under the hot sun each day.

'I do hope she's not going to embarrass herself over that boy,' she says after a minute, raising her sunglasses. Will, who is still standing beside me, takes so long to answer that at first I think he is not going to bother.

'In what way?'

'I would have thought that was pretty obvious,' says Susie coolly, lowering her sunglasses and lying down again. I glance up at Will. He is staring out to sea, his face impassive. 'I thought you'd be pleased to see her looking happier again,' is all he observes.

'What?' says Susie, who clearly had considered the discussion to be at an end. 'Oh . . . well, naturally, just so long as it's not the prelude to more misery. We could all do without that.' I hear the click of her lighter and the woody smell of cigarette smoke is in the air, the drawing in and letting out of a breath. My eyes are half-closed to reduce the glare from the water and I ought to be considering this new tension but I am still thinking of fingers pressing down on me, can feel the height of Will rising up above me, the breadth of his back and shoulders – so different from the thin, well-remembered shapes his body used to make. Joe too is starting to thicken a little as he gets older, but his bones are still slight and angular and I have always been drawn to this neat European quality of his, have rarely been attracted to men whose chief characteristic is an overwhelming maleness. There is, I remind myself, something repellent and brutal about solid muscle slung across dinosaur-thick bones, and yet the sun is hotter than ever today, beating down on my skull and confusing my thoughts, and suddenly a kind of madness is upon me, making me imagine how it would be to accommodate the weight of this man, of Susie's husband. I stare down into the water; make myself peer into its coolness. Grains of sand shift and resettle around Will's feet and a tiny, almost translucent fish darts around his heel, butts at it and seems to nibble, but he doesn't appear to notice anything.

'An odd way of looking at it, don't you think?' he says and his voice is a hot thump of panic in my brain and some kind of defence is nearly falling from my lips before I understand that I have not spoken anything out loud, that Will is still talking to his wife. Then he is gone, wading out a few paces and disappearing beneath the water in a shallow dive. When he emerges, a sleek lion's head in the swell, he is beside his daughter.

*   *   *

'You seem better,' comments Joe, lying on the bed with his hands behind his head, surveying me with the beginnings of interest as I come out of the bathroom, still naked from my shower.

'In what way?' I say, though I have already noted the same thing. Days of good food and idleness have taken the gaunt, worried look from my face and added curves to my hips and my breasts. I look younger, more promising.

'More relaxed, I suppose,' says Joe with a yawn. I check my reflection in the mirror and begin to dry myself, though it is hardly necessary in this heat.

'I suppose it felt like an adventure of sorts, going off by myself the other day,' I observe.

Joe frowns. 'I thought you said it was just over the hill?'

'Yes,' I force my voice to remain light though it wants to tighten. 'But it's the kind of thing I'd forgotten how to do, so it made me feel I might be able to go on with it. Now that I've started again.'

'Good,' says Joe with an approving nod, reaching for me. Instinctively, I slip away from his grasp.

'Not now,' I say.

CHAPTER 20

As I lie in bed that night, I let my mind drift. I envisage Will disappearing beneath the water again and then the shape of him rising up out of the waves next to his daughter. Then I close my eyes and think about being out on the terrace with Milly, and how, one morning when I am plaiting her hair, I might tell her about a summer in England, a lifetime ago, when the skies were a dirty yellow and a haze of hot pollution caught in your throat each afternoon.

Hannah has disappeared to sports camp and my mother leaves the house to teach summer school every day, returning when the sun is setting fire to itself among the oily swabs of cloud over the tops of the terraces, or later still, after I have gone to bed.

My mother has spent all of our money in anticipation of this summer-school salary, so nothing has changed: people still come knocking at the door, wanting to come in and discuss bills that cannot be paid, and the fridge is still an empty mouth, humming pointlessly to itself. With Susie in Ireland, there is no one ringing frantically on the doorbell (always having just heard – how, I am never sure – of some party or gig that we cannot possibly miss, striding across to my wardrobe and demanding to know what, exactly, I intend to wear), forcing me out of myself in a way that I pretend to resent but secretly rely upon. That last holiday in Greece has fooled me into thinking that I need her less, but at home in Daycliffe I miss her more than I thought I would, wonder all the time what she is doing in Ireland, and wish I had thought to ask for her grandmother's phone number so that I would not now be waiting, day after day, for her to call me. From a distance, this summer after exams had looked like a freedom waiting for me to reach it, but I had failed to understand something fundamental: how hours without structure slowly start to fall in upon themselves.

Days drift into nights where I remain for the most part alone – my mother often going straight from class to the pub or to a restaurant with her new students. I go for walks among the terraces after dusk, restless as the heat of the day dies, thinking that I should almost certainly look for a summer job, for at least then I could pay a few of the bills that are scattered across the kitchen table and these weeks of summer would have to arrange themselves into some kind of order, could no longer keep on dissolving into one another. But by the next day the decision will seem to have atrophied into an impossibility and I am helpless again, almost frightened by the way time can empty itself of everything. There is so little food in the house that the effort of putting this right begins to seem too irksome. Weight falls from my bones and I am less scared than before because I know that it is only me that could have made this happen and that I have not lost all control of these hot, collapsing days.

Each evening the shadows of the terraced houses close in on either side of me and I wonder where Susie is right now, wish she was here to make light of this for me, to steer me round to seeing that it is not me, or us, but the world which is at fault. I try to picture her, make her voice reach me, but I have never been to Ireland or met her relatives and it is hard to find her in these unsatisfactory nights when there is no sound but the echo of my footsteps on the hard pavement and the only movement the odd, dark shape of a cat clambering over plastic rubbish sacks, seeking a small adventure of its own. All the way home I expect something bad to happen, almost willing it to come:

a figure slipping out of the darkness, a hand across my mouth, the knife in my back.

'Is this just about you?' Milly might interrupt. 'Or did my mum come back from Ireland?' I imagine her to be impatient this day, scanning the bay beneath us for Michaelis's boat though it is far too early to expect him.

'Wait,' I'd tell her.

One day the phone rings and it is not the gas or electricity people wanting money but Maxine, a girl I had just begun to know at school. Her voice is full of laughter and as light as air and I do not bother telling her about these long days of solitude in this empty house because she would only wonder why I hadn't picked up the phone, would never understand that such a thing never even crossed my mind as a possible response. Then she asks me if I would like to come to a party at the weekend and I thank her and say yes and wonder what she can be thinking, inviting such a dark contaminant force into her happy girls' world.

It is not the kind of party to which I am accustomed, no anonymous, bare-boarded house with unbanistered stairs and couples locked together in darkened bedrooms, but a proper party, for Maxine's birthday, at her parents' house. Unaccountably, people seem pleased to see me and in the days that follow everything changes because Maxine and her best friend Helen and all their other friends seem to like me more than I'd have thought possible, and there are times to be had that I'd never before considered: games of tennis to be played on the hard courts in the local park, train trips to the seaside, afternoons spent sunbathing on the smooth, green lawns of the houses where these girls live. There are some familiar points of reference – the usual talk of boys and clothes and sex – but they remain peripheral always, brief diversions from the heart of the matter, and these days slip by so full of innocent enjoyment that they seem to me to have been plucked from the pages of the school stories I read as a child. I could pity these girls their sheltered upbringings, try to envy or dislike them, but it would make no difference to them for they are as embedded in their world as I am in mine. I cannot tell Milly – whose face is already setting into accusation as I relate this – but in many respects I find those girls easier company than Susie for whom so many things – so many seemingly innocuous people – are utterly intolerable that you always have to think twice before ever owning a liking.

Helen is rounding people up one day, organising a welcome-home gathering at the pub for her brother, who is coming down from Oxford. Having already met a few of her male acquaintances – boys from the local grammar or from the minor public school on the edge of town – and been less than impressed by them, I take little notice of the proceedings. I am used to working-class boys in the main, tough and cool beyond their years, not these Marcuses and Benedicts, whose gawky bodies and arduously long anecdotes take up more space than they could possibly warrant. What's more, I have only just finished reading *Brideshead Revisited*, can't help imagining Helen's brother to be some stuttering, effete Anthony Blanche-esque creature, some hateful little fop of a boy. I do not even bother to turn up at the pub the night he is due home and so it is not until a week later, at a barbeque in someone's back garden, that Maxine says: 'That's James over there, Helen's brother,' and she points to a boy standing by a bench on the far side of the garden. James is, after all, perfectly normal looking, clearly a little older than everyone else at the party and unmistakably related to Helen. But something else is immediately nudging at the edge of my field of vision, like a needle pushing through a cell membrane beneath a microscope. My gaze slides away from Helen's brother towards a wiry, auburn-haired boy who is standing beside James offering him another beer. A shock goes through my nerve ends, like recognition, like pain before it arrives.

'Who was it?' Milly would say, her head jerking round because I have come to a sudden halt.

'The boy with the auburn hair?' I'd say, carefully finishing a plait. 'Oh, that was your father.'

CHAPTER 21

I swim while Susie sits on the edge of the pool, sunbathing and half-watching Milly and Michaelis fight over a lilo. Samuel has plucked up just enough courage and is hovering in the shallow end of the pool, having first checked with me – a fellow coward – whether this is advisable. I am floating on my back when I hear a soft moan and out of the corner of my eye I see Susie slump forward. When I reach her she has her elbows on her knees now, is running the tips of her fingers over her brow, pushing upwards towards her hairline as though she is trying to lift a weight. Beads of sweat – or is it water from the pool? – shine on her top lip.

'I'm OK,' she says.

'What is it?' I ask, looking up at her anxiously.

'Nothing,' she says with a smile, wiping her forehead. 'Just the heat. Maybe a touch of sunstroke.' But Will insists on taking her over into the shade of the umbrella and then going up to the villa to fetch some water. When he returns, he bends over her solicitously for a few minutes, seems to be apologising for something, though the heat cannot be of his doing and Susie has never once complained about it before.

'They don't seem to feel it so much any more, do they?' I say, nodding towards Milly and Samuel, who are playing around with some badminton rackets and a shuttlecock at the far end of the pool terrace with Michaelis. Susie and I are sitting, immersed up to our necks in the water, hardly moving except for slow anemone-like waves of our hands and the odd bobbing motion to maintain our positions. Susie shows no sign of her earlier distress.

'Alexia says it'll be even hotter before the week's out. It hardly seems possible, does it?' Susie tips back her head into the water, closes her eyes, and lets her legs drift up to the surface. After a moment I follow suit, because though it is still morning and the cypress trees are fresh green points spearing the sky, the sun is driving down into my scalp. We hang in the water, as if waiting for an invisible current to take us somewhere.

'Are *you* OK?' says Joe later when everyone else has gone up to the villa for a siesta and the two of us are lying side by side at the pool's edge. It is days since he pushed me away from him in the olive groves, but I understand that we are not talking about the heat or cases of sunstroke.

'Yes.'

He reaches for my hand, strokes the back of it with his thumb.

'I think we needed this holiday.' By which he means that there is still a chance that everything might get better. A happier silence than those we have known these past few days settles over us and our hands remain lightly linked as we lie there, feet dangling in the water and the sun hot upon our skin.

I open my eyes a little, look out across the bay. Today the sea is a slow, congealing mass.

'We should go somewhere together,' I say. 'Just the two of us.'

The next morning, Will comes to the breakfast table with a map in his hand, hanging half unfolded.

'I thought we could drive up to the mountains,' he says, dropping down beside me and opening up the map across the table. 'I reckon we're all going to start climbing the walls if we don't get some respite from this heat soon. The kids are refusing to come of course but,' he points at the map, 'it should be cooler up there.' Susie joins us, fresh from the shower, her hair sleek against her scalp and her blue kaftan washed and ironed. Already it is hard to remember her slumped over at the poolside yesterday.

'That's the highest mountain,' says Will, indicating a point on the map. 'You remember me telling you about the firs that grow there, Alice? There's this little road running all the way up and the guidebook says there's a picnic area somewhere. I thought we could drive up and have a bit of a walk, take a picnic maybe, and then drop down to the coast again and find somewhere to swim.' Susie is nodding vigorously in agreement, watching the lines that Will traces out on the map and looking less inward than she has done in last few days, and Joe is already suggesting places we could stop to swim, but something bad is pushing up in my throat.

'But should we be leaving the children here? All alone?' Everyone looks at me and nobody speaks for a moment. 'I mean,' covering my presumption, 'I'm just asking. That's all.' These are not my children to protect.

'Samuel isn't a baby,' says Susie, 'and Milly is quite capable of taking care of him.'

'I've told them they're not to go out in the boat,' reassures Will.

'It wasn't just Sam I was thinking of . . . ' I begin and then give up because it is clear that my feeble dissembling has fooled no one.

CHAPTER 22

Leaving Milly and Samuel with instructions not to leave the immediate area of the villa, we drive down the track and join the main road, turning towards the village where we plan to pick up from the supermarket the extra food we need for a picnic. Susie sits beside me, her head leaning against the window. Joe is in the passenger seat beside Will, puffy-eyed and pale because he drank too much wine last night and more handsome because of it. I watch his profile and wonder for a second whether the past is too thick between us for me to believe in this beauty of his any more. Even as I think it, I know that it is a pointless question to ask myself. The answer can make no difference when the two of us are tied together in knots grown so tangled and messy over the years that separating us would require a courage more clinical and determined than either of us possesses.

'What's that noise?' he asks suddenly. Susie and I tilt our heads to one side.

'What noise?' says Susie.

'The engine. It doesn't sound right.' We listen again and hear what Joe has heard: the engine seems to be working harder than it should be to take us along this easy coastal road. Will winds down his window and drives more slowly, listening all the time. When we pull up at the village quayside, five minutes later, a small wisp of smoke is rising from underneath the bonnet.

'I'll leave you to go to the supermarket I think,' says Will, pacing around the front of the car and frowning at it.

'I'm going to have to get Dimitri to take a quick look. I don't want this thing breaking down on us up in the mountains.' He gets back into the car, drives the short distance across to the little travel-agency office on the other side of the road and parks outside. By the time we return from the supermarket, with fresh bread and six bottles of water wrapped together in thick plastic, he is handing over a set of keys to Dimitri, the owner of the agency and the representative for our holiday company.

'No go,' says Will as we approach. 'Dimitri wants to take it into the garage. We have to wait while he makes a phone-call and then he'll run us back to the villa.'

'There's no other car we can use then?' asks Joe.

'Nope. Everything's booked out,' says Will motioning towards the kerbside, where only a row of scooters is parked.

Susie peers around the door of the travel agency at Dimitri, who is leaning back in his chair, gesticulating into the phone.

'Shall we go for coffee?' says Will with a shrug. 'I have a feeling we could be here for a while.' We walk in the direction of the first café in the row that runs along the quayside. Susie stops and turns to me.

'Why don't we take out some of those?' she says, pointing back the way we have come.

'What?' I ask.

'Why not take out some scooters?'

'I don't know how,' I say quickly.

She raises her eyebrows. 'How difficult can it be?'

'They're pretty dangerous,' says Will intervening.

I am reminded of a day many years ago, Hannah and I lying on a beach in Corfu and suddenly everyone on that beach looking the wrong way, not towards the sea, where children play in the mild blue waters, but up at the cliffside, and when we follow their gazes we can see nothing except what look like two scraps of white material caught on the rocks, flapping in the wind. It is only later that we learn that two young English girls on a moped have fallen to their deaths, have ended their brief exploration of the island by driving round a blind corner and right over the edge of that cliff. 'They don't even give you crash helmets here, I notice,' he adds.

Susie laughs. 'Oh don't be such a scaremonger, Will! Why shouldn't we take them out? I'm not going back to the villa again. Not now you've brought us here,' and she turns away from him, is looking at me again and her eyes are wide open, sharp as stones and fully awake, the way they used to be when we were young and she'd come marching down the pathway to my house, hammering on my door, standing there on my doorstep vibrating with the possibilities waiting out there for us.

'What do you think, Joe?' says Will doubtfully. 'I could ride one myself. I'm just not sure it's such a great idea . . .' Susie sighs aggressively and shifts from one foot to the other. Joe shrugs, says he doesn't mind, that he has ridden a scooter once or twice before, when he was a kid, not wanting to be the one to face down Susie when she has this reckless, almost dangerous look on her face. She turns her back on us, walks swiftly across to the row of scooters and stands in front of them, expectantly.

She looks at me. Will and Joe look at me. My imagination is already working up scenes of blurred terrifying exposure, of big things outside the delicate layers of my folded-in world. On the boat nearest to this end of the quay, a man and a woman have a map spread out on the roof of the cabin. The man points at something, seems to be asking the woman a question. She shades her eyes and looks up, at the sky or perhaps out to sea. Except for a few gossamer-like wisps of cloud on the horizon, the sky is empty of every-thing. I picture us – Joe and me, then Susie and Will – on board those insubstantial-looking scraps of metal, parked outside the travel agency now, but in my mind seen from a distance, two hard-bodied insects, with pink limbs poking out at skewed angles, whining along a mountain road that twists ever upwards, like the thread of a screw, and all around a bright blue nothing, a vacuum wanting to be filled. Susie's gaze does not leave me and then, just as I am about to protest, something enters her expression which goes beyond a mere desire to compel – *For Christ's sake, Alice!* – a kind of naked pleading in her eyes, and I am so startled to see it there that I find a voice inside my throat that is bigger than I'd imagined it could be. I look at Joe, but he is looking down the quayside, thinks he knows what is coming next. I smile, a hard, unbreakable smile

'Shall we?' I say.

CHAPTER 23

'All sorted,' says Will, bounding towards us. 'We've got those two beauties on the end' – he points at a pair of white scooters. 'Where's Suse?'

'Just coming, I think,' says Joe, looking over to the quay-side, where Susie has gone to buy cigarettes. She is smoking one now, staring out across the bay. The smoke hangs in the motionless air, which is already heavy with heat.

'You're OK with this?' says Will, looking at me. I nod and then look away for a moment, feigning interest in some clattering coming from a delivery van which has pulled up outside a nearby restaurant. I clasp my hands, holding myself together.

To onlookers, our pace through the village must seem ridiculously slow. Will and Joe take time to familiarise themselves with the scooters – turning the accelerators tentatively at first, slackening off rapidly when the machines lurch forward, trying again, a little more gently this time. When we are clear of the houses, we start to speed up and I can only cling to Joe's back, eyes half-closed in terror, wanting and not wanting to see what is ahead of us, and the road beneath my feet a blur, for the coastal road is busier than I'd expected it to be: lorries and buses and the occasional tourist coach swinging unexpectedly round corners, bearing down on us with great sucks of air, before disappearing in clouds of dust that hover in quick memory and then drift back down to earth. It is a relief when, after a short time, we follow Will and Susie on to a smaller road heading inland where there are no cliffs falling away to the sea beneath our feet, no wide air waiting to swallow us up.

This road is narrower than the coastal route but its surface remains remarkably good. We ride through straggling villages where women shade their eyes and watch us pass and old men with skin the colour of hide sit unmoving in *kafenions*, past small patches of cultivation before the villages start to peter out. Once, Joe has to swerve suddenly to avoid an unidentifiable mess of feathers and blood at the edge of the tarmac, and the farther we travel the more it becomes apparent that this road is only a faint line of civilisation through the wilderness. On either side of it, the ground immediately breaks up, loose piles of cream-coloured rocks and stones that would tear your skin to delicate shreds banked up on either side of us, holding back the dry scrub where cicadas scream in some eternal protest and, beyond, the sudden swell of the hills, at the feet of which erratic boulders lie. It is waiting to close in again, this wilderness, to heal this thin man-made wound, and I am reminded of Delos, where man's small efforts are slowly crumbling to nothing among the grasses. I loosen my grip on Joe's T-shirt a little – just as a pick-up truck appears out of nowhere, roars straight out in front of Susie and Will from a dirt track at the side of the road, forcing them to swerve violently to avoid its back end. The scooter wavers and then rights itself and a shout of laughter reaches us. Susie tosses her head, turns, and motions to a road sign ahead, her hair streaming out exultantly behind her. A dark peak rises up in the distance. From here, it looks like the flank of some great, implacable beast. The thought of weaving our way up its sides makes me cling to Joe again.

There is scarcely any other traffic on this road, just one or two hire cars driving carefully past us, and, with the exception of some kind of military emplacement halfway up the mountain, no signs of habitation. The small engines of the scooters have to work harder now, pulling us up the ever-increasing gradient, and after a time the last of the tarmac passes beneath our feet, giving way to rough stone. We judder over bumps and dips and swerve to avoid pot-holes but I can see that up ahead this road becomes thickly wooded, right up to the apex of the mountain, and that these trees will soon contain us, protect us from sudden exposure and yawning air wanting to pull us over the edge. On and on we ride, more slowly now as the scooters' engines fight the ascent and the road gets more and more ridged and potholed, and as we slow the heat closes in around us again. When I lay my cheek against Joe's back, sheltering my eyes from the rising dust, his T-shirt is soon dark with sweat that could be mine or his.

Will raises an arm – the scooter wobbling for a moment – and motions to the left, before turning into a break in the trees. The engines die and silence and dust settles around us. We are on a lagoon-shaped plateau, a car park of sorts, where two motorbikes sit in the sparse shade to be had at the edge of the clearing and a couple of swings and a seesaw have been erected, some half-hearted attempt, swiftly abandoned, to provide a children's play area in this dustbowl.

'I thought we were going to the top,' says Joe.

'This was the only car park marked on my map,' says Will. 'I think you have to walk the rest of the way. It can't be far from here.'

'But the road doesn't end here,' protests Susie, hopping off the back of the scooter and, shading her eyes with one hand, looking up through the trees. Her flip-flopped feet sink into the rust-coloured sand that makes up the surface of this car park. Will is taking the map from the mesh side-pocket of his rucksack, tracing a finger across it. I glance down at myself, see that my legs are finely coated in dust. I could be a statue coming to life, half-human already. Or perhaps it is the other way round and the dust is rising up to enclose me, a thick red blanket that soon will stop the breath in my lungs.

'Well, it does go a bit higher,' admits Will. 'But you know I'm not sure these scooters are up to it.' He motions to them. 'You really need a four-wheel drive on this kind of road.'

'Well, we haven't got one and the whole point of coming was to go to the top,' says Susie.

'Honestly, Suse,' says Will, shaking his head. 'I don't think it's a good idea. We don't want to get stranded up here if one of these gives out on us. We're miles from anywhere and there's no guarantee someone'd pass by to pick us up.'

'Then why bother coming at all?' Susie kicks the dust with her toe and looks determinedly towards the road we have just left and for a moment I see Milly in her, or her in Milly, a connection that seems oddly incongruous.

'Let's walk,' says Joe, swatting at a fly that is bothering him. He takes a long swig of water from the bottle we packed in the rucksack, blinks into the light and frowns. 'It's too hot to argue.' And indeed it is, for though it may be marginally cooler up here, the air seems to have snagged itself on the trees, presses down upon you so that no matter how deeply you draw it into your body, you cannot seem to get enough oxygen into your blood. We park the scooters next to the motorbikes, a meagre token of companionship in this wilderness, and with rucksacks loaded on to our backs set off towards the road.

It is past midday and within minutes we have come to a halt, everyone breathing heavily though the car park is still visible behind us.

'We'd be better off walking through the forest,' suggests Will. 'At least we'd be in the shade.'

So we try climbing up from the road and making our way through the trees but there are no trails marked or, at least, none that we can find, though Will insists that this is walkers' territory, that he'd read all about it and that there must be signposts somewhere. We clamber over tree roots and rocks, trying to find a way upwards, Susie's feet slipping out of her flip-flops and making her stumble and me managing more than once to turn the same ankle I weakened clambering up the rocks from the wild place. Every time we find some kind of pathway leading upwards, it peters out after a few hundred yards, or we find our way blocked by undergrowth too thick to negotiate. The trees are all around us, holding us tight among them, and there seems to be no obvious way up and no way out into clearer air. The heat dulls my brain and I can think of nothing, except keeping going. Sweat is running down my back – making my shorts and T-shirt stick to me – and between my breasts. Insects swoop in upon us, whining in my ears or settling on my skin.

'I give up,' says Susie quietly. I am the only one who hears her and that in itself may be a mistake, for the words seem to be for no one. She is standing quite still behind me, her shoulders slumped and her chin resting on her chest.

'There must be a way to get to the top . . . ' I say, pretending not to notice her defeated stance, remembering how much this seemed to mean to her, back there in the car park. She raises her head slowly and then spreads her hands out in supplication.

'What's the point, Al?'

Her face is pallid beneath the film of sweat and it is clear that the climb has been too much for her, but there is something else too. I wonder what she was expecting to find here.

'Over here!' comes a voice from up ahead.

'They've found something!' I say excitedly, like a child. Then I hold out my hand like a coaxing mother. 'Come on!'

Will and Joe are standing in a clearing. Behind them the trees fall away down the mountainside and far, far in the distance is the smoky blue of the sea.

'How about *this* for a view?' says Will with a sweep of his hand, as if he has personally arranged it for us: those tiled rooftops far beneath us; that curve of land down towards the coast; the sea that is so far below us that is seems not to move. We all stand and take in this gift of his, forcing soupy air in and out of our ribcages until our breathing slows a little.

'Probably doesn't get any better higher up,' admits Joe. He drops his rucksack. 'Shall we eat here?' And we all agree, though you can hardly feel hunger, or anything else, with this thickness pushing down your throat.

The minute we start unwrapping the food, the whole forest comes alive, outsize flies and wasps and unfamiliar flying insects bearing down on us, thick-bodied and thuggish, like nightmare caricatures of their English relatives, settling on our sweat-sodden clothes, on our sticky skin, buzzing past our ears and trying to find their way on to the food even as we lift it to our mouths. The village bread we are chewing on has already started to harden and the ham – which was already too shiny and a suspicious shade of bright pink – is unpleasantly warm and floppy. When I open the cheese I find it has run into a gluey yellow mess that has almost to be poured from its plastic wrapping. Ants appear from the undergrowth, finding their way along the fallen tree trunk where we have perched.

'So these are the firs that Odysseus used,' says Will, turning his head with slightly too theatrical an air of wonder to observe the forest from which we have just emerged. I follow his gaze out of politeness – everyone else is too disgruntled to bother. When I was in amongst these trees I had forgotten all about them being the very species used to build the boats that carried men to Troy. Joe smashes his hand against his thigh and leaps up.

'Little fuckers bite!'

Will puts a piece of bread down next to the ants and

immediately they break ranks and swarm over it.

'You could get eaten alive in this place,' says Joe, throwing the rest of his food down into the undergrowth and watching as the wasps converge on it. 'No one would ever know.'

'Oh they would,' said Will brightly. 'I told you, this is walkers' country. It's in every tourist guide. Can someone light a cigarette? It might keep the insects at bay. Did I tell you about the horses that live up here?'

'No,' says Susie in a weary tone. She has recovered her colour now but she has not attempted to eat anything except a few cherries for lunch. Will appears not to notice the edge in her voice.

'There's a herd or two of them apparently. The villagers used to let their work horses graze here, but during the Second World War they were left to run wild.' He grimaces at a fly, throws the remains of his bread to the ants, and then goes on. 'The incredible thing is that they are actually descendants of Alexander the Great's horses. They're related to the Pindos horses which come from north-eastern Greece – his neck of the woods, so to speak – but because of their isolation they've become a separate breed altogether.'

'Can we see them?' I say, a little thrill running through me at the thought of Alexander, that blank-eyed statue, and the hot flanks of horses shining on the plains of Persia.

'Probably not,' says Will. His voice becomes lower. 'The herds are extraordinarily shy – the merest sight or smell of humans and they disappear into the trees.' I feel my stomach tighten for a second. The hint of intimacy in his voice is as if he had just touched me. 'Then again,' he continues, his voice returning to its usual volume, 'We might be lucky. Perhaps we should have another look around after we've eaten . . . '

'Oh, for Christ's sake, Will!' interrupts Susie, getting to her feet. 'Stop trying to make everything better all the time! Can't you see everyone's had enough now?' She spins round, turning her back on us all, gazes out to sea, but I can see that she is trembling with rage. Joe and I stare down at the ground.

'But . . . I *would* love to see the horses if we can.' I venture.

'It was a bad idea, coming here,' says Susie flatly.

'Will's already told you that they bolt before you can get to them,' Joe reminds me. 'Why don't we drive down to the coast instead?' He stands up and stretches, looking out towards the motionless sea on the horizon. 'I could do with a swim.'

'Good idea,' says Susie.

'OK,' says Will, equably. 'Whatever everyone wants.'

Susie throws a few of the picnic things into her rucksack and then lifts it up on to her shoulder and stands waiting, her mouth set tight, barely able to contain her impatience with the rest of us as we clear away the remaining scraps of food and any other evidence of our presence here.

'Can you take a look at the map, Susie?' says Will, glancing up at her. 'If we keep going on that main road, I think we pass by a place called Metaxata, or something like that. Byron lived there for a time just before he joined the Resistance. There's bound to be a taverna or something there. We could stop . . . '

But Susie is gone, away into the forest, back the way we had come.

After a minute or so, we catch up with her but let her stay in front, setting the pace, because it is clear that this is what she needs to do. Eventually, we step out of the forest again and make our way back down the road, blinding white after the green canopy of the trees, to the car park. It is a cauldron of heat in the afternoon sun and the sand slips inside our shoes, gritty and burning.

'I want to drive,' says Susie. She is standing in the partial shade, where we left the scooters. The two motorbikes have gone and already the sand is covering over the faint imprint of their tracks across the car park. 'Alice can come with me.'

'But you don't know how,' points out Will.

'I do. I learned years ago.'

'You've never said.' Will eyes her, carefully.

'Why would I?' says Susie with a shrug. 'A boyfriend of mine had a scooter. He taught me how.' She turns to me. 'You remember Matt, don't you, Alice?'

'I'm not sure,' I say because it was always hard to keep up with all the people passing through Susie's life, or rather, with the lives *she* passed through, and then there were all the others I never met, those who lived elsewhere, in the secret world she inhabited whenever the notion to escape took her. For a second I think Will is going to do something stupid, like asking Susie to ride across the car park on the scooter in order to prove her capability to him, and in my head I am pleading with him not to because Susie has that look on her face, the one that used to settle there just before she disappeared for a day, or a week at a time. Instead, he tosses her the keys.

Susie was not lying. She starts up the scooter first time, and after I have settled myself behind her, sets off across the car park and out on to the road without a wobble. Will and Joe follow us out, and the four of us head down the mountain again, slowly at first to avoid the worst of the potholes, then a little faster as the road becomes smoother. The sun is high in the sky now – siesta hour – and no traffic passes. Even the cicadas seem muted, their screeching reduced to a muffled hum in the foliage on either side of us. I can discern the beauty of this mountainside now that there is cooler air whipping against my skin, awakening my senses again. I hold lightly to Susie's waist as we travel over the bumps and think that it is a dark, secretive place, this forest, that is does not give itself up to you readily. It is a place to come alone, not in noisy, picnicking hordes, crashing through the undergrowth and expecting it not to resist your presence. I wish that we had happened upon the horses though, seen, even just for a fleeting second, the swish of a tail or heard the skitter of hooves, fleeing. We hit a pothole and Susie accelerates out of it. The motion pulls me backwards, forces me to remember my grip. The scooter shudders over the loose surface of the road, but instead of easing off again, Susie increases the speed still further. I say nothing, waiting for her to slacken off, but a moment later she accelerates again and I crane around, see that we have pulled away from Will and Joe, are bowling down the hill at some rate.

'Slow down a bit,' I ask, leaning forwards to reach her ear. My voice judders and wind blows into my mouth, sucks away its moisture in an instant. We are travelling far too fast now, almost as if the scooter is running away with itself, Susie's black hair flying into my face. Quickly, I glance behind me again: we are losing Will and Joe, and Will's bulk, sitting at the front of that other scooter, looks suddenly vulnerable, too small against this brutal landscape.

'What are we doing?' I shout, pulling at Susie's shoulder, but she does not notice me at all, and we are whizzing past the trees and over the blurring ground. We swing around a sharp corner and I see ahead of us, see that very soon we will be emerging from the trees and will have no more protection from rock-strewn slopes falling away beneath us. Ideas are flipping through my head like animation: something is wrong with the brakes, the accelerator is stuck, Susie has lost her senses. I remember that great leap from rocks to shingle, in the wild place, wonder if I could do it again, right now. From behind, shouting, the whine of another engine.

'Susie!' I grab at her shoulder again, risk shaking it. She wriggles free from my grasp, hair streaming like a flag in the wind, and there comes the unmistakable ring of laughter on the air.

'Slow down!' I plead, my knees gripping tight. I turn, see

that Will and Joe have managed to gain on us. Something then catches my eye, something moving in the trees. Later, I will think that I heard the crackle of dry wood in the undergrowth, but it must be a trick of memory because the shouting and the engines drown out any nuance of sound.

'The horses!!' I scream but even as I do so I think that I may be wrong because that swift moving thing among the trees, too fast to be human, appears to be flesh-coloured. Susie's head turns, following where my finger points, and I am glad that, at last, something has broken into her madness, or is it mine, breaking into hers? She is too late though: that swift moving flesh has been swallowed up by the darkness and there is only the screeching of tyres and metal and more shouting and then here is the blurred ground, suddenly seen with intense clarity, coming up to claim us.

CHAPTER 24

The world is a distorted mirror, bending and then shattering into bright shards, as vivid as stained glass. Then everything is still again and I am on my side, awash with thankfulness for the blue of the sky above my head and the feel of the dry scrub against my skin, knowing that all of me is certainly intact. It is strangely peaceful, lying here – almost comfortable with the noise of the cicadas purring in the grass all round me, clearer than ever before. Nearby, a lifting of metal and then an indistinguishable kind of groaning. Another movement, hurried this time, and the next thing Joe's face is looming over me, dark against the blue sky.

'Are you OK?' he asks. He is crouching, breathing heavily, as though he has been running. Sweat glistens across his nose. 'You must have been thrown clear.'

I nod. Then, my eyes are drawn to a long streak of blood on his shirt. I push myself up on my elbows. 'You crashed too? Are you OK?'

'Yes, except my arm,' he says, holding it out in front of me. The damage is on the outer side, where he has tried to break his fall, a cut running all the way from his wrist to his elbow. It doesn't look to be a deep wound but it is a messy one, with gravel and small greyish stones embedded in the flesh, beginning to turn scarlet now as slow blood wells up around each piece of debris. 'The scooter's had it.' I nod my head. I can see it lying in the road, twisted, and there is Will, shaking himself off and starting towards us.

'Susie?' I say to Joe, but before we can move, Will has passed us, is sprinting towards the scooter upon which, only seconds ago, Susie and I were travelling. It lies on its side now, wheels still spinning, a short distance ahead.

I look for Susie but no other movement disturbs the horizon and now I am moving too, towards that frame of road and sky, everything speeding up and Joe running beside me.

She is lying on her back in the middle of the road and as we approach I find myself worrying about things that don't matter, like why we didn't spot her straight away. After a second my brain understands that the scooter was blocking our view. Will glances quickly back in our direction, raises a hand as if to stop us, and then bends over the scooter, starts lifting it from where it has fallen. Joe takes hold of my arm. The glinting metal of the scooter wants to blind me, but my vision is suddenly sharp and even from this distance I can make out the loose weave of Susie's kaftan, the wind casually picking at the flimsy blue material. Her face is turned away from us and her hair is spread across the dusty road.

'Will?' The cicadas pause for a moment and my voice is unnatural, a sacrilegious noise in this hushed place. For a second I fear that the odd silence will swallow us all up and then I see that Susie's body is stirring. I step forwards in relief and then come to a sudden halt, sweat rising in the small of my back: something is wrong. Susie twitches, and then seems to convulse.

'Will!' I call, my voice shrill with fear and he is standing up now, turning around and walking towards us, fast. I think that he is going to speak, seize me by the arms, but he carries on past. I let him go, pull myself free from Joe's grip and force my legs to go forward, cold fear in my veins. Just as I do so, Susie convulses again, turns her head in my direction and I see that her face is contorted by laughter.

A roar grows from somewhere nearby, shaking the still air.

'Car!' says Joe. Susie makes no effort to move, just clutches her stomach in another spasm of silent laughter. Will passes me again, is beside her in a second, dragging her to her feet and virtually lifting her out of the road. He half carries her over to the side of the road, his face straining with the effort. There is no time to move the scooters before a blue car bears down upon us, dust rising from its tyres.

'What the fuck are you playing at?' Will snarls as he deposits Susie on the roadside, his face ugly with sudden rage. He glances back at the car, which has managed to pull up sharply just before reaching us. 'Trying to get us all killed?'

'No, no,' says Susie. She is still gripped by laughter, holding on to a tree trunk to support herself and seemingly impervious to both her husband's fury and the uncomprehending stares from Joe and me. 'Just myself,' she says solemnly and I think that something of the wildness of this place must have found its way inside her after all, up there on the mountain, or that some window into madness has suddenly been shattered, and I am frightened for her.

'I'm *joking*!' she says, at last seeming to register our concerned faces.

There is the slam of a car door, a voice calling, and Susie must be dizzy with laughter or shock because she loses her balance and stumbles against the tree trunk. Once again, her face contorts and next she has slumped to the ground with her hands covering her face. After a moment I realise that she is no longer laughing but crying. Joe looks away, towards the owner of the car who is approaching. Will and I do not move. 'My foot . . . ' says Susie, looking up and wrestling for control of her facial muscles. She points to her right leg. Her skin is suddenly grey.

'What have you done to it?' asks Will, dropping to a squat beside her, his voice softening.

'I don't know . . . but when it caught the tree just now . . . '

Susie closes her eyes and leans back against the tree trunk, her face almost unrecognisable with pain. A second later she is on her knees, retching into the scrub.

The car driver is a Greek named Nikos who speaks English with a pronounced Australian accent. He offers to drive us to his brother's taverna in the next village from where, he says, we can telephone the travel agency. Will and Joe help Susie into the back of the car and five minutes later we are sitting around a wooden table in a small roadside taverna, where the village elders gaze at us in open curiosity, calling across to Nikos from time to time to make enquiries, whilst a girl who might be Nikos's daughter or niece serves us cups of thick black Greek coffee. We are a sorry-looking party in all – Joe with a bloody arm, Susie with her swollen ankle, and all of us with road-dust in our hair and limbs covered in grazes and scrapes. Nikos shakes his head and goes off to his house to fetch his wife.

Susie has recovered herself by now and when Maria, Nikos's young wife, arrives, armed with bandages and some kind of ointment which, she signals – for her English is less fluent than her husband's, will help to reduce the swelling, she is happy to sit with one leg outstretched on Maria's lap, smiling beatifically at the dark-eyed village children who, catching the baleful eye of Maria, dare not step inside the taverna itself, but hover at the edges, chattering to one another in gruff tones and beckoning to friends. When Maria is finished she fires a warning volley in throaty Greek at one or two of the bolder children who are edging past the first row of wooden tables, and then disappears inside to fetch more coffee, Will following behind her, in search of a telephone to call the travel agency. When he comes out again, ten minutes later, Susie is attempting to explain: ' . . . You know when somebody falls over in front of you, or when you're a child and you hear that someone really ancient has died? And there's something so . . . so ridiculous and . . . undignified . . . about them *letting* that happen.' She looks at me and at Joe, to see if we are getting this. 'Maybe you've always suspected that there was something ridiculous about them anyway . . . '

I laugh out loud, enjoying the insult.

'What's that got to do with us crashing?' says Joe, frowning at me.

'Well, I'm not exactly sure, it just felt the same. I suppose I had a vision of how stupid we looked, sprawled across the road like that, our smug little day trip all messed up.' Susie begins to laugh again. I have to stop myself from joining in and I wonder if we are both still in shock.

'Not so funny really,' says Will flatly, standing over her. 'Somebody could have been dead for all you knew.'

'Oh, Will – '

'Why didn't you slow down when I shouted out to you? What do you think the children would say?' Will lifts his hands to his forehead and rubs it, agonising. 'Jesus, it's the sort of thing we should be warning *them* . . . ' he tails off.

Joe mutters something about it being nobody's fault or everybody's fault and no harm's been done.

'Of course,' says Susie to her husband. She turns to Joe, touches his hand and smiles ruefully. 'I'm so sorry about your poor arm, Joe. It's completely my fault.'

Joe waves away her concern and Will walks off for a moment, stands at the entrance to the taverna and looks up and down the road as if expecting someone, though not a single car has passed this way since we arrived. After a minute he comes back.

'Dimitri's coming with a pick-up van but there's only room for two of us to ride with him, so I said we'd bring back the other scooter ourselves.'

'Why not put both of the scooters in the truck and get Nikos to call a taxi for us?' asks Susie.

Will sighs in exasperation. 'Because I didn't think of that at the time and because we're causing everyone enough trouble as it is! I thought the best we could do would be to get at least one of the scooters back to Dimitri in one piece.'

'I'll wait here with Susie, shall I?' I say brightly, trying to cover for Will's irascibility.

Susie grins at me, untroubled by her husband's temper. Then she looks at Joe. 'But your arm's a real mess,' she says in a regretful tone. 'I'm not sure you'd manage to ride all the way back.'

'I *am* having trouble bending it,' Joe admits, holding the damaged arm out to demonstrate, half-enjoying the novelty of injury. I suspect that he would prefer to sit here in the sun with a cold beer, waiting for Dimitri, instead of trekking back along the dusty road to the scooters.

I look at Will and he at me. His expression is affable again but he looks wearied by the events of the last few hours, suddenly seems older than the rest of us, and I am reminded of the day he collected Joe and me from the airport, how the breadth of his body seemed somehow insubstantial against the backdrop of this island.

'Just you and me then,' he says.

CHAPTER 25

That summer, I understood for the first time how one person – drinking beer on the other side of a garden, or wherever else you find them – can raise you up above all of the mess you have accumulated around yourself until you seem to float above it, a remote, faintly heard world whose air you no longer breathe, where everyone moves like puppets on invisible strings.

Will has auburn hair, long narrow limbs and shoulders which have not yet broadened into manhood. You can see it there though, a strengthening waiting within him. He has pale skin with a pink bloom beneath it where the blood runs close to the surface and when he scratches his nails over it, as he does from time to time, pausing between collecting beer glasses from tables to bother at the gnat bites that are inevitable down here by the river, long scarlet welts rise up on his forearms or the backs of his hands. He should be in India with his girlfriend right now, but he broke up with the girl, just like that, found himself at a loose end for the remainder of the summer until James – with whom he works on the university newspaper – invited him home. The two of them find work at the Waterside Inn – a large family pub-cum-restaurant that is quiet enough for most of the year but does great business in the summer months due to its location and the cheap steaks and burgers it churns out of its kitchen all day long. James helps out in the kitchen and Will, who has worked behind a bar before, serves drinks and meals to the customers, moving among the tables with plates of steak and chips and precarious, high-stacked burgers in his hands, with an easy confidence, deferential to all the customers.

Will doesn't bray and bawl like other boys. He is softly spoken so that you have to lean in towards him if you want to catch every word he says. Will draws you into intimacy without even knowing what he does and I notice how the other girls flush a little when they speak to him, their voices growing higher with excitement though he singles out none of them for special attention. The landlord of the pub tolerates the rest of us so long as we don't move around *en masse* bothering the other customers, who arrive in small motorboats or park in the vast tarmacked car park on the far side of the pub. The Marcuses and Benedicts come sometimes because they look up to Will and James, can see where they themselves might be in a few years' time, but often it is just us girls sitting at one of the picnic tables in the garden each evening, drinking Malibu and pineapple juice beneath the sweet, decaying smell of fried onion rings blowing out from the kitchen ventilators. On the surface nothing has changed: I am quiet mostly and then, occasionally, loud and cynical, making the other girls laugh, but all the time, out of the corner of my eye, with the nerve ends in my skin, I am waiting for Will.

My spiked hair and the ripped clothes I used to wear have gone by now but I am no more approachable than before. Just before Susie went away to Ireland, both she and I had our hair cut in the style of Astrid Kirchherr, the photographer who transformed the Beatles' image in their early days in Hamburg and whose iconic self-portrait, cool and artistic, we both love. Susie's hair falls easily into this style, but mine is coarser and stubbornly kinked and it takes me hours of work with a brush and hairdryer each morning, smoothing, smoothing away at my rough surfaces until they gleam. I am a hard, polished creature, in sleeveless high-necked dresses run up on Susie's sewing machine, flat winkle-picker shoes that jam my toes into unnatural shapes, and old ladies' cardigans, which I find in musty bins in second-hand shops and wear the wrong way round, with the buttons running down my back.

But Susie is gone for the summer, gone away when she could have insisted on staying at home, and I am left here alone, a dark oddity among Helen and Maxine and the other girls all dressed in their summer clothes, their light cotton skirts and T-shirts in sherbet colours. Together, they are a posy of flowers, handfuls of prettiness, so light and airy, so *accessible* beside my hard lines that they could flutter into someone's arms and that person would barely notice. None of this is new to me but until now the differences between us never mattered.

After hours, when the cars have emptied from the car-park and James – red-faced from an evening turning steaks in the sweltering kitchen – brings out beers for the two of them, you see another side to Will. He and James undo the top buttons of their shirts and take long greedy gulps of the cold beer. Then you can see them starting to relax, the violet dusk falling down around all of us as we sit on the quayside, darkening the water beneath our dangling feet. Soon Will becomes sharper in his observations, more boisterous, quick shouts of laughter bursting out of him as James describes some disaster in the kitchen that evening, the two of them pretending to fight, clinging on to each other and rolling precariously close to the water's edge, so that the black shadows of water birds start up and panic on the surface of the river in the coming night. Will treats the girls in our group with a kind but casual affection, yet with me he is cooler, never holding out a hand to pull me up from the grass or slinging his arm around my shoulder. His seeming indifference stings me more than I could have imagined and once or twice I appal myself by being pricklier than ever in his presence, making the odd cutting little joke about privileged backgrounds or ivory towers, and then loathing myself when he responds with no more than an uncomprehending look. I live in terror that I will be discovered – for how can anything so tangible remain undetected? – and found risible, and in even greater terror that Will may leave this place, slip away from me at the end of the summer without ever knowing. The thought of this riverside, this pub, this life, without Will in it now seems a desolation too painful to contemplate and I am filled with a mixture of abhorrence and envy for his life in Oxford – a place that, in my imagination, is Will and perpetual sunlight through trees, punts easing forward through cool, green waters.

Our house fills up for the summer with vague groupings of people on their way to music festivals or dreadlocked couples stopping off early on a road trip to somewhere or other, and sometimes they stay for a day and other times they are still here, weeks later, parked around our kitchen table with their rucksacks stacked against the wall, the thick smell of marijuana caught in their hair and their dogs barking in our yard. Hannah is home from sports camp by now and these houseguests warm to her open, youthful face, her happy nature, but they find me harder to fathom. One in particular, a boy improbably named Simeon who can be only few years older than me at most, seems to regard me as some kind of mental exercise, prodding at me for some sign he can recognise. He remarks on the neatness of my appearance, draws everyone's attention to the time I spend in front of the mirror in the hallway each morning, blow-drying my wild hair into submission, says that there must, surely, be a man involved. Once he has taken the trouble to point this out, all of them are happy to tease me, these friends of my mother's, believing my carefulness to be some kind of *petit bourgeois* affectation, a manifestation, perhaps, of my essentially suburban spirit. I say little, but inside I despise their blurred, messy edges slumped over our kitchen table and chairs, pity them because they do not realise that even Simeon, the youngest of them, is old and tired and far beyond any kind of pain or beauty, would not understand that you can hold these things within you without anyone knowing.

In the quiet hour or so when the Waterside Inn first opens and few or no cars have drawn up outside, Will often sits behind the bar reading, or scribbling in a notebook, one foot propped up on a bar stool, jumping up to serve people when they arrive. One night, I say: 'What are you reading?' Every word new in my mouth, awkward as a pebble lodged against my tongue, my teeth.

'Ezra Pound,' says Will, flipping up the cover of the heavy volume for me to see. 'For my dissertation.'

'Oh?' I say in a tight little voice.

'He's a bit hard going at times, but worth persevering with.' He holds my gaze but there is wariness in his eyes, as if he is waiting for some form of judgment to come down upon him, and it is my fault because my longing for him has made me even harder and more polished around him, when all the other girls have fluttered and flirted and tried to charm.

'Oh.' I shift my eyes to the optics ranged behind the bar, pretending to deliberate.

'What are *you* reading at the moment?' he hazards, and I am so thrilled to learn that he has noticed something about me – the books always stuffed in my bag, under my arm – that I find myself flushing like a child and my mind emptying itself of all sense.

'Just this and that,' I mutter and I turn to go, pretend that I have changed my mind about wanting a drink after all, managing both to confirm the aloofness of my nature and disprove my reputation for a smart mouth in one easy step.

At home, I try to escape my mother's friends by staying in

my room, lying on my bed and concentrating on Will – the warm, alive smell of his skin brushing against mine by mistake, the spade-like outline of his hands, long-fingered and capable and too big for the rest of his body – but one of the hippy types has given my mother some wind chimes which she has hung by the kitchen door and the incessant whimsical jingling of these chimes in the summer breeze – silvery and supposedly charming – finds its way into my brain even when I have the window tight shut and my room hot and airless. Soon, that fairy-like tinkling will begin to drive me crazy, forcing me out of the house and on to the streets, where I walk for hours, the heat striking up from the cracked pavements and my shoes pinching my toes. If I forget to replace the plasters on my heels before I leave the house, those shoes will rub my skin raw, the blood running down my heels and soaking into the lining fabric, but I do not stop. I walk into town and back again and sometimes round in circles, half-blinded by the sun, street after street, like a hamster on a wheel, for, though it may be hours till evening falls and I can legitimately present myself at the Waterside Inn, this mere act of putting one foot in front of another makes me feel as though I am walking towards Will.

CHAPTER 26

We leave Susie and Joe in the taverna, say our thanks to Nikos and his wife and refuse a lift back to the scooters.

'They've done enough for us already,' says Will, as we walk the short distance out of the village and over the hill. He strides out, grim faced in the heat of the afternoon, and I am like a small child running behind him, trying to keep up. It is a relief when we arrive at the site of our accident, where we find the scooters as we left them, lying in the dust at the side of the road like a couple of discarded toys. Will crouches down and checks both of the scooters once again, but it is clear that only one of them is in anything like working order. He props the other up against a tree, brushes some of the dust from it for appearance's sake, and then wheels the functioning scooter out into the road.

'Come on then,' he says, seeming to notice me for the first time.

In the beginning I hold on lightly, but soon I am forced to adjust my grip for safety's sake, though I manage to maintain a kind of distance by holding myself stiffly, my arms a rigid semi-circle around his waist.

'Are you OK?' he asks once, slowing a little.

'Fine!' I call, too brilliantly, make myself soften against him. We pass through one or two villages and the occasional car flies past us, but for a time it is really just the two of us, moving steadily forwards along this country road, the sun hot upon our backs and the high whine of the engine circling us. It is the first time I have been alone with him, truly alone like this, and I hold it to myself tentatively, unsure of what I am to do with this unexpected prize.

'Where are we going?' I ask, tapping his shoulder. Will has taken an abrupt turn off the main road, on to a dusty track.

'I saw a signpost back there on the road.' He points ahead and through the trees I see a small taverna. We follow the path that threads through the trees and Will brings the scooter to a halt, switches off the engine. Greek music, with its compelling eastern wail, snakes in our direction.

'Dimitri will be ages picking up the others,' he says, turning to me. 'And I could do with something to eat. How about you?'

Beneath the deep shade of vines, we drink cold beer and eat stuffed tomatoes that sit in pools of thick green olive oil and, we agree, taste better than anything we have ever eaten.

'Must be the near-death experience,' I joke and then wish that I hadn't. 'Oh come on, Will,' I say as his expression darkens again. 'It was an accident.'

'Yes,' he says with a sigh, pushing his plate to one side and leaning his elbows on the table. 'I'm sorry.' After a minute: 'I was so bloody livid, that's all. Such a stupid thing to have happened.' I nod, drink the last of my beer and, thinking he is done with the subject, am about to ask him something about his work. 'I thought she was dead, you see. When I was going to her.' Will's voice is low. He stares down at the table. 'I didn't know whether I'd have the courage to touch her.'

'Susie's fine,' I say, wanting to reach across the table to him but not daring to do so. 'She always is.'

'But what was she was thinking of?' His eyes are suddenly fierce, staring into mine.

'I'm not sure I know. Maybe it was just – '

'I would have to have gone back to the villa and . . . ' his fists clench. 'Can you imagine, Alice?' The waiter hovers, sensing a bad moment. Will smiles at him and, after we have dealt with the bill, apologises to me. 'I'm sorry, Alice, it's absolutely fine.' As we get up to go, he adds, 'If only she'd stop to think sometimes.'

Then we are busying ourselves with rucksacks and getting the scooter started again and so it is only when we are back on the road, the dust rising up around us, that it occurs to me that after all these years Will hardly seems to understand his wife at all.

All the way back along the coast road I cling to him, this time moulding my body to his, my face resting against the warmth of his back and the engine thrumming up through his ribcage and along my cheekbone. I can feel Will's shoulder blades through his T-shirt, can see up close the vulnerability of his neck and the white skin of his scalp as the wind parts his hair. Behind us, obscured by the dust, are Susie and Joe, and the maze of minute, intricate connections and complications they represent to the two of us. I close my eyes and breathe in, filling my nostrils with the clean, warm smell of Will, blocking out everything that is ahead of us – the children waiting at the villa, the intractability of a future locked always in the past, that tangled mess of loyalties and habit and adult responsibilities. Soon the unchanging landscape begins to have a soporific effect on me and I have to remind myself to hold on tightly, find myself thinking that this road might go on for ever, that we could just keep on going, driving and driving, and yet be suspended in time, and I am just starting to believe it, judgment also suspended, when the pitch of the scooter's engine alters.

We are on our own dirt track, passing the sign for the Villa Stamatia, instead of continuing on the coast road.

'I'll leave you here,' explains Will a few minutes later,

when we have pulled up outside the villa. 'There's no need for both of us to wait around in the village.'

'Oh,' I say and desolation must be in my face for he reaches out and takes my hand in his, making me start.

'Don't worry about anything, Alice,' is all he says before turning the scooter around and accelerating away from the driveway.

I stand and watch him go and then make myself grow calm. Samuel's baseball cap, which never stays on his head for more than five minutes, is lying on the drive. I pick it up and brush the dust from it before entering the villa. I almost expect to see the children lined up on the sofa, awaiting my arrival with an air of disapproval, but no one is in the living-room or out on the breakfast terrace. I go from room to room, stepping quietly in case anyone is sleeping through the heat of the day, but though there is evidence of food having been eaten in the kitchen – the bread knife on the board, crumbs scattered across the floor and a pile of unwashed plates in the sink – and Samuel's bed looks to have been slept in, I find no one home.

Even before I get to the pool, I know that it is too quiet. No splashing of water, no bickering, no music from Milly's CD player (the headphones that her parents insists she wears when she listens to her music sure to have been removed at the first opportunity). I am about to turn back up the steps when I do hear something: the sound of glass, falling but not breaking, a smothered giggle. I go to the bottom of the steps, turn the corner and walk out on to the terrace. The sun is glaring off the surface of the pool and I see nothing for a second. But there: movement. In the far corner of the terrace, in the shade of a tree, a sun bed, bare flesh.

'Milly?' I call. A bottle on its side, the green glass glinting in the sunlight as the contents spreads like a bloodstain across the paving. The tangle of limbs becomes two people and Milly and Michaelis spring upright in an instant, their faces blank with shock. They are, I am relieved to see, clothed – if you can count swimming costumes as clothing – but the straps of Milly's bikini are around her shoulders. I walk slowly across the pool terrace, deliberately giving myself – and them – time.

'When did you get back? Where are the others?' gibbers Milly, tugging frantically at her bikini straps.

'It's all right, Milly,' I say, trying to sound calm. 'It's just me. But your dad will be back soon so I think Michaelis had better go now.'

'We weren't doing anything . . . ' begins Milly. Michaelis, looking red in the face and less self-assured than ever before, says nothing. I look closely at the two of them, at the wine glasses beside the sun bed and the spillage on the paving. Neither of them can have drunk a great deal and yet Milly is having trouble focusing on me.

'You should go and have a shower, Milly. The water will sober you up.'

She does not move. Her eyes are wide with fear. 'Are you going to say anything to my dad?'

'We'll talk about it later,' I say, uncomfortable with the responsibility she is foisting upon me. 'Go on!' I order, as authoritatively as I can manage. After a parting glance at Michaelis, Milly scuttles away.

'I should clean up this mess,' says Michaelis, bending down to right the wine bottle.

'No,' I say, thinking that all this will feel more manageable once he is gone. 'I'll do it.'

'Will . . . will everything be OK?' asks Michaelis uncertainly.

'I don't know,' I say shortly. Something else is wrong. 'Where's Samuel?'

'Up at the house,' says Michaelis. Then, seeing the way I am looking at him, 'Oh, we didn't send him there, I promise. He just got tired of the pool.'

'No,' I say. 'I looked everywhere.' I think of Samuel's room, his comic books all askew across the bed, but no Samuel. Then the other bedrooms, the empty kitchen, the living-room, the terrace. I think of the baseball cap, lying in the dust, and then something cold is beginning inside me, the beating of dark wings at the edge of my field of vision.

'Check the house again,' I order Michaelis, though I am sure that Samuel is not there. Michaelis does as he is told, running up the terrace steps, two at a time. I follow him, stand in the middle of the driveway, panic thumping so loudly in my brain that, for a second or two, it drowns out all rational thought. I clench my fists, force myself to think clearly. If Samuel is not by the pool and he is not in the house . . . I cross the driveway to where the long, dusty track leading to the main road begins. There is no one in sight and I cannot imagine any impulse that would persuade Samuel to set off in that direction. I think again, try to push away the image of the baseball cap lying in the dust. We should never have left Samuel alone here. He is too young, too frail. The only other place I can think of is the beach below the villa but Samuel cannot swim, won't even paddle in the shallows since the incident with the sea urchin, so there is no reason why he would go there. I cannot stand here another moment just doing nothing. From inside the house, I can hear Michaelis calling for Samuel. I set off into the olive grove at a run.

*　　*　　*

My breath is coming hard in my chest by the time I reach the cliff path. I go straight to the edge and lean out over the stone wall. There is no time to think about exposure today. Below me, nothing. An empty bay. I look again, scanning from side to side, and then I see it, out by that first rock, something pale bobbing just beneath the surface of the water.

'Oh Jesus, no, please no,' I am gabbling to myself. I am running the way I used to run when I was a child, my knees trying to reach my chest, and still the path keeps on stretching out in front of me, switching around a corner, stretching out in front of me again, and then at last shingle is flying under my feet.

'Samuel!'

And there is movement in that water again, a white arm rising, and I am running towards it, the water trying to hold me back. Another arm rising, a face, half-submerged, pale against the water.

'Samuel!'

Then a reedy, triumphant voice.

'I'm swimming!'

I wrap Samuel in my arms, hold him close to me though he does not want to be held, keeps trying to break away from me.

'I did it! Did you see me? I can swim!'

'Oh Samuel,' and I make him sit down at the water's edge and then walk away for a moment, force myself to stop sobbing because I will frighten him.

'Shall I tell you exactly what happened?' Samuel is behind me, making me jump. He is alive with himself, cannot sit still for a minute.

'Tell me later,' I say, but he is brimming over.

'We were just sitting around the pool all day and no one wanted to play with me, so I went back to my room and they came looking for me and I was pretending to be asleep and then I really did fall asleep and I dreamt that I could swim . . . ' And I try to hush him but all the way up the cliff path and back through the olive grove I cannot stop him talking.

CHAPTER 27

Over dinner that night we pretend to be ashamed of what happened today, all of us agreeing that it was foolish to take the scooters out in the first place, but even Will's voice has a swagger in it now that we are all safely back at the villa, and we keep on laughing and checking our injuries and shaking our heads in wonderment. In a strange kind of way, the accident has woken us all up, provided us with something that was missing.

We eat out on the terrace because it is the coolest place to sit, Susie pouring wine for everyone from the heavy, earthen pitchers she bought in the village. Earlier, before everyone arrived home, I drew Milly and Samuel into the living-room, sat them both down on the sofa, and made them promise that the swimming would be kept as a surprise, that nothing is to be said just yet. I need not have concerned myself about Milly – she says barely a word all the way through dinner – but Samuel is hardly able to contain his new secret, insists on sitting opposite me at the table and keeps trying to catch my eye, his glances teasing and conspiratorial. Once, though no one has addressed her, I notice Milly flushing, and I am convinced that she is thinking about my voice, shrilling across that swimming-pool this afternoon. I am still angry with her for the responsibility she has handed me, a responsibility I did not seek, and yet . . . a moment which should have been frozen in her memory, as delicate and perfect as a snowflake, has been sullied. By me. Suddenly I remember how it felt to be young and to crave just one cool, clean space in the world, unpolluted by adults, or, at the very least, some kind of neutral ground where your feelings and wishes would carry equal weight.

'I'll help,' says Milly, jumping to her feet as soon as I start to clear away the plates.

'You seem to have acquired a surrogate daughter,' remarks Susie.

Someone has opened the windows in the kitchen, trying to disperse the heat from the oven, but still it is unbearably hot beneath the strip lighting. Milly puts down the plates she is carrying, rests one hand on her hip and lets the other one hang loosely. I can see sweat breaking out through the powder that coats her cheeks.

'It's OK, Milly,' I say, in what I hope is a calming manner. I smile, but Milly is suspicious of me. OK is the sort of thing an adult might say to make you feel better and then you find out that their version of OK doesn't match yours at all, that they're going to do exactly the opposite of what you want them to do.

'What do mean, "OK"?'

'I've been thinking about this all afternoon,' I say as quietly as I can, not wanting my voice to carry out on to the terrace. 'You see, Milly, I'm in a difficult position because your parents are my friends and so I guess I'm responsible for you in a way . . . ' I hesitate. 'On the other hand, I do remember how it feels to be your age and . . . ' My hands are running through my hair, lifting the weight of it off my face. 'Look, I hate having to say this to you because it's nothing to do with me really . . . but I have to ask you to be careful. You must know . . . '

'I knew you wouldn't tell anyone.' The muscles in her face have softened. She's not about to be grateful though. 'Not that it's anyone's business but mine and Michaelis's . . . ' she lets that hang there for a second, as if challenging me, anyone, to dispute the conjoining of their names, ' . . . but if you really want to know, we've decided not to do anything like that. It wasn't how it looked.'

'Good,' I say, relieved. I bend down to open the dishwasher, start loading the first of the plates into the bottom rack.

Milly sits down nearby on a chair. 'I wish I could get away from everyone sometimes, that's all.'

I glance over my shoulder at her. Again, that prettiness in waiting, almost hidden. A thought comes to me, is out of my mouth before I've had time to process it. 'Maybe *we* could go somewhere.'

'What?'

'The two of us. Go off on an adventure of our own. To Ithaka or somewhere.'

Milly stares at me. 'What, for the day, do you mean?'

'Maybe,' I say, casually.

'Why?'

I take a hold of myself. 'I wasn't being terribly serious.' I change the subject. 'About Michaelis. It's just that your parents – and your mum in particular – are bound to worry about you, you know . . . ' I am talking lightly now, for the sake of it.

'No way!' The tone of her voice makes me flinch. Milly is right behind me, standing over me. She stares down at me, a look almost of menace on her face. In this awkward, half-crouched position, loading the last of the things into the dishwasher, I feel suddenly vulnerable. 'You must know that's crap.' Milly's mascara is melting into her eyes. The heat in this kitchen is almost intolerable. 'I wish . . . I just wish you and everyone would stop *pretending*, that's all!' says Milly, shaking her head as if she is trying to butt the heat away from her, 'My dad worries about me, I know, but not *her*, not my mother.'

'But that's ludicrous, Milly. Just because you've had some little argument . . . ' I say, standing up straight and stepping towards her very carefully.

Her jaw is clenching, she is fighting for control of the muscles in her face. 'You think so?' she says, looking straight at me, defiant. 'You're supposed to be her friend, aren't you? You did practically everything together, you said. Then maybe *you* can explain to me why, exactly, she tried to abort me?' I am motionless, but something unstoppable is boiling up inside Milly. 'Did you all think I was stupid or something?' she spits.

'Milly, I swear . . . I never knew . . . ' I move towards her, my arms open, and for a moment I think she is going to collapse into me, a child falling into my arms.

'I don't want to talk about it any more,' she says, her voice suddenly dull, and then she turns on her heel abruptly and is gone.

CHAPTER 28

I take my copy of *The Cantos* of Ezra Pound to the desk, feeling as I do so that no one in this library – that middle-aged woman browsing the local-history shelves, that pensioner tapping experimentally at a keyboard, peering at the screen in front of him as though it is some kind of dangerous miracle – can be unaware of the motives throbbing in my veins, flooding my skin: *I love him, I love him.* And in the days that follow – when evening is a long time coming and it is too dangerous to walk by the Waterside Inn more than once or twice during the day, seeking the shape that Will's body makes among the crowded tables – I lose myself in poetry. Page after page of *The Cantos* proves too dense with historical reference for me to make any sense of it, or simply impenetrable because the wanderings of this troubled mind lead me in circles, but I understand enough, can't help feeling – with the presumption and self-aggrandisement of youth – that Pound's fragmented world somehow chimes with my own, that my own need to impose some kind of order on the chaos of my life before Will came (before Will came!) is comparable with Pound's futile attempts to form everything into a whole.

I copy out the myth of Actaeon who, I discover on another trip to the library, was transformed into a stag and torn apart by his own hounds for daring to spy upon the huntress goddess Artemis as she bathed naked in the woods:

> Beneath it, beneath it
> Not a ray, not a sliver, not a spare disc of sunlight,
> Flaking the black, soft water;

Bathing the body of nymphs, of nymphs, and Diana,
Nymphs, white-gathered about her, and the air, air,
Shaking, air alight with the goddess,
Fanning their hair in the dark . . .

Spotted stag of the wood,
Gold, gold, a sheaf of hair,
    Thick like a wheat swath,
Blaze, blaze in the sun,
    The dogs leap upon Actaeon,
Stumbling, stumbling along in the wood,
Muttering, muttering Ovid . . .

And when I reread it I am reminded of Delos, the birth-place of Artemis, remember how something of her invincible spirit found its way inside me as I walked among the ruined streets of that island. And because I am in love with Pound's visionary words and with Will I make these words, these *worlds* I find within the pages of *The Cantos*, into an understanding between us, though I live in fear that my feelings might be exposed to him, transmute from something delicate and secretive into a daub upon a wall, crude and violent in the light of day. The weeks are passing quickly, too quickly. Sometimes I hear Will and James talking about the autumn term, their plans for the newspaper, but now that this poetry is shared between us I feel certain – *almost* certain – that something will happen, though what that something might be I cannot say, for I can see no circumstances in which I might speak out. But this line lifted from Pound: 'What thou love'st well shall not be reft from thee', I make mine, holding it close to me, turning it over in my head as I lie in bed staring up into the dark; it is a mantra circling within me.

One Sunday, it is so hot that James borrows his father's car and a crowd of us squash ourselves into the back and we set off towards the coast, with music on the radio and everyone in a holiday mood. When we arrive, an hour later, we find that the rest of the world seems to have woken up with the same idea: everywhere you look there are fathers hammering windbreaks into the sand – though there is not a breath of air – or setting up umbrellas, and whole families of beach chairs are arranged within these little enclaves so that reaching the sea front is like making your way through a maze of canvas. We stay there for a while, crammed together right at the water's edge, wandering in and out of the half-hearted waves now and then, but more and more people keep arriving, with towels and radios and picnics and fractious naked infants and it is a relief when James suggests we drive on, continue down the coast until we find somewhere less crowded.

The beach we come to has no name so far as we can tell, but it is a vast buff-coloured stretch backed by dunes and almost empty except for a few beached fishing boats and one or two lone figures along the water's edge, walking dogs that bound in and out of the sea every few minutes. It is exposed here and cooler, the air moving more freely, bending the grasses that cling stubbornly to the dunes and stirring the surface so that here and there, out of the corner of your eye, you discern minute avalanches taking place. If you stand still for a moment at the top of one of these dunes, as I do while James and Will are trying to decide where best to park the car and Maxine and Helen cross to use the small block of toilets on the other side of the road, it begins to seem as if it is alive beneath your feet, sand running away all around you. After a minute, the others climb to join me and then we let our feet run away with us, slipping and sliding down the far side of the collapsing dune.

The chill of the sea and a briskening wind bring us all back to life after the morning's torpor and soon we are taking it in turns to paddle out, face down, on the body boards Helen and James brought with them, thrashing our legs as fast as we can and then turning when the right moment comes, and letting the waves, which come in cold brownish-green rolls, surge us back towards the shore. Clouds pile up in the sky, covering the sun, and the wind blows stronger as the day goes on, the waves starting to rear up and then crashing down on to the shore and fizzing and foaming in your ears as you are carried along. Once, a wave lifts me higher than ever and then dumps me unceremoniously on the wet sand at Will's feet and he reaches out his hand to me, pulls me to my feet. Later we warm up by playing football but the wind is wild now, keeps catching the ball and taking it into the waves. The wind streams through my hair, whipping it across my face, between my teeth, and I know by tonight it will be a tangled mess, but the wind and the waves have torn something loose in me and I am like someone who does not care, haring after the ball like a child, wrestling with Maxine when she tries to tackle me, a new energy running through my limbs. Another time, James kicks the ball in my direction but it is a wild kick, the ball curving off towards the dunes. I tear after it, my feet flying across the sand, but just as I reach it Will is there on my shoulder, trying to slide his foot in front of mine. I pull back but it is too late and the sand is coming up at me and Will has fallen too. The two of us lie there for a second, winded and laughing, before we scramble to our feet.

'Your hair looks pretty like that,' says Will suddenly. And his hand reaches out and his fingers are pushing through my hair, which hangs in waves around my face, stiff and heavy with salt.

'Thanks,' I say, staring at him. My face flushes and I do not look away or try to hide it. And in my head: 'What thou love'st well shall not be reft from thee.'

CHAPTER 29

Midnight is long past when I switch on the bedside lamp again. I try reading for a while but I cannot stop thinking about Milly: eyes that seemed to be both accusing me and pleading with me at the same time, conferring on me a new responsibility that hangs over me during the long and silent hours that come when everyone at the Villa Stamatia sleeps.

Joe is hot and restless beside me. He wakes once, complaining of a headache and nausea. I fetch him water and some painkillers and switch off the light. The painkillers do their work and soon he is sleeping more peacefully, arms flung out on either side of him and the scar on his inner arm – caused by a fall from a tree in childhood – silver in the moonlight. I watch him for a while: the gentle throb at the base of his neck, the blue branches of veins at his wrists, where the skin is thin and fine-grained, think how life has to keep moving or die, of that vital passage of blood from lung to muscle and organs, so easily damaged. The delicacy of the mechanism. My thoughts darken as I recall a night long ago, Joe coming home late when I am already in bed, cold and resentful between the sheets, and him with blood on his shirt and on his knuckles, explaining that he'd got into a fight with a drunk on the train home. The confrontation was unavoidable, he'd said, and the next day I'd pleaded with him to take more care in future, picturing nightmare scenes where cold steel flashed into his soft, warm flesh leaving me all alone in the world. But rather than disturbing him, the incident appeared to have excited Joe, put a glitter in his eye and deepened his breathing, and only weeks later the same thing had happened again, or something very similar. That time he came home with a split lip, had to make up a weekend football injury the following Monday at the accountancy practice, and I was angry with him because he seemed too ready to give up on himself, almost as if he'd been expecting to fail all along. Eventually, I sleep. When I awake, my book is lying on my chest and bars of fresh sunlight are coming from behind the shutters. Joe stirs beside me.

'I feel ill,' he says.

I fetch him more water, keep the shutters closed while I dress.

Outside Will and Susie's bedroom, I knock and wait.

'Come in!' calls Susie. When I enter, she is standing in front of the mirror, drawing her black hair into a knot at the back of her neck. Will is lying on the bed reading a book, wearing only a pair of shorts.

'I think I'm going to have to put a new bandage on,' says Susie, indicating her bound foot, which is swelling over the top of the dressing and turning a shade of indigo round the edges. 'This one's already starting to look like something from the Crimean War.'

'Can I speak to you?'

'Sure,' says Susie brightly, waiting. My eyes travel to Will and she understands, slips outside the door.

'What's up?' she asks. She squints into the fierce light as she follows me out on to the breakfast terrace where the canvas canopy has yet to be pulled across. 'God it's hotter than ever.'

There is no easy way towards this. If there had been, I would have found it during the sleepless hours of the night. 'Milly told me something awful yesterday,' I say.

'Oh Jesus,' says Susie, the light smile falling from her like a stone. The muscles in her face have frozen. Then she shakes her head in puzzlement. 'No, you can't mean that. How would she know yet . . . ?'

'No, no,' I say hurriedly. 'It's nothing to do with Michaelis.'

Susie closes her eyes for a second, her face relaxing. Then she opens them in a decided fashion. 'What then?'

'Something she must have overheard before you came away,' I say slowly. 'An argument between you and Will, I would guess . . . '

'Oh, she's been bleating on to you about all that!' says Susie, cutting across my careful words. I stand very still, thinking that the world must have skewed itself while I slept.

'I thought there must have been some . . . ' I try to think clearly. 'You knew about it? That Milly had found out, I mean?'

'Yes, of course we did,' says Susie brusquely. 'Milly's hardly one to keep things to herself.'

'But . . . ' My brain is still trying to catch up with the madness of this, to put all of these images into some kind of new order. 'When did all this happen?'

'You just said it yourself. Before we came away.'

'No, I don't mean that, I mean the abortion –' I can't find the right word – 'attempt.'

Susie looks at me and for a second I think she is going to drop her jaw and let her eyes roll in her head. Pull the retarded face we once used to indicate irredeemable stupidity in another. 'When d'you think?'

I frown, cursing my mental slowness. 'Before you left Daycliffe?'

'Yes, of course. Look, it's a long time ago now but it's pretty simple,' says Susie impatiently. 'I didn't want to be pregnant – as you must have known – and I tried to do something about it before it was too late. Will persuaded me to think it over for another few days and in the meantime he announced the good news to our families. I wasn't exactly delighted about any of it at the time.' She gives a little shrug. 'Will and I were having a bit of a fight a few weeks ago and for some reason it came up. We hadn't talked about it for years, as it happens, and Milly turned out to be in the next room when we thought she was in the garden.'

'Oh.'

'I tried talking to her before we came away.' A door opens somewhere nearby, closes again, neither of us takes any notice. 'But I can't tell her it's not true, which is what she's really after.' In the blaze of the sun out here on the terrace, we are like two players upon a tiny stage. 'Oh,' says Susie, when I do not respond. 'Not you as well.' She stares at me. I have disappointed her in some way. 'I wish everyone would leave me alone.'

'But Milly came to me,' I say. We carry on staring at one another across the terrace, gazes locked. 'What I can't understand is why you didn't tell me at the time!' I blurt. 'I thought we were friends . . . ' My voice is pathetically small and wavering and I am horrified by my own selfishness, the realisation that the hurt I feel on behalf of Milly is dwarfed by that I feel for myself, for the girl I once was. Susie studies me for a silent moment.

'Oh, Alice, what could *you* have done?'

*   *   *

I step outside with no thought for protection, no hat, no T-shirt over my bikini and shorts. Beyond the shade cast by the walls of the Villa Stamatia, the sun waits, ready to prey upon any soft-bodied, water-bound creature that ventures out into its glare, to suck living juices from spongy flesh, searching out the dry framework of life. I cross the driveway, take the path to the beach, the olive grove giving me respite from the worst of the heat. Just as I reach the fork in the path, I hear footsteps coming fast behind me.

'Slow down a minute,' calls Will as he reaches me. He puts his hands on his hips whilst he recovers his breath, and I watch a drop of sweat run from the crook of his elbow – soft, still pale skin – down his forearm. It is the heat that does it. Makes the smallest exertion feel like walking through water. 'Are you all right?' he asks.

'Yes,' I say and turn round and keep going, not continuing on the beach path but taking the fork which leads deeper into the olive groves. I can feel the invitation hanging in the space I have left behind me, a high-pitched bat squeak of possibility. For a moment there is silence, and then foot-steps following.

Will says little until we have reached the far side of the bay, beyond the low white house and the vegetable patch that belongs to Michaelis's grandmother, where all is quiet today. Then: 'I'm trying not to be angry with her too.'

'I'm *not* angry,' I say truthfully. The anger has gone, leaving the thought that I must always have misread this friendship with Susie, foisted myself upon her from the very beginning. But then . . . always Susie calling, out of nowhere. Months of silence in between, but still . . . Always her.

'It's just so hard for Milly, the poor love,' says Will. 'You can't take back those words once they've been said.'

'Susie must understand the damage that's been done,' I say, swinging round to face him. I am remembering Milly's face, a child's howl of pain gathering there but never surfacing, and I'm suddenly furious, more so than when Susie was standing in front of me, her presence somehow complicating everything.

'You'd think so,' says Will. 'Before we came away she promised she'd put things right. She thought Milly needed time to cool down first.'

'I never knew anything about this, you know.' My voice is hard, protecting myself.

'It's a long time ago, Alice,' he says in a reluctant kind of way. I nod and start walking again. I set off up the hillside and Will follows me, not questioning where I am leading him. After a moment, he says: 'Susie had been acting strangely.' I wait for him to draw level with me and he keeps his eyes on the ground as we start to climb. 'Kept going back to the doctor's even though the pregnancy had been confirmed and she seemed well enough. Every time I tried to talk about the future she'd go along with it but her eyes would have this look about them, as if she was elsewhere.' A lizard flickers across the stony path in front of us and Will comes to a halt for a second, stares down at the space where it had been. 'I can't remember all the details. I think Susie said she was going to stay with a friend – might even have been you, thinking about it – and I looked in her diary and found an appointment in there for the same day. I didn't know where this place was she'd written down or quite *what* it was, so I pretended to go along with it all . . . '

'You followed her there?'

'Yes.' We stride out the last few paces, reaching the crest of the hill. A hot breeze blows here, winds itself around our dusty legs and through our hair.

'I'm tired of all this – being in the middle of Milly and Susie all the time,' says Will. 'It's hardly happy families.' He drops down to a sitting position on a small rock, resting for a second, and for a moment I can see how the impossible will happen, how the thickness of his skin and the clean lines of his profile will begin to dissolve and he will become old. 'Christ, sometimes I think that I got it all wrong, Alice, thinking we could keep going after that. I don't think that she's ever stopped hating me for preventing that termination. And now, poor Milly . . . '

'And you still want another child?' I kneel beside him, my legs folded beneath me, not caring about the stony soil digging into my skin. A dark patch has risen on his T-shirt, down the centre of his back, and I think that that is the exact spot where my head was resting yesterday. I would like to stop talking about Susie now, lean into him and draw the scent of him into the dark cavities of my nostrils.

'Susie's told you that?' Will looks at me. 'I suppose it seems mad in the circumstances, but I come from a big family myself, you see, and it's not as if we can't afford it these days.' He gets to his feet again, holds out a hand to pull me up from the ground. I am suddenly aware that I am semi-naked before him, my shoulders and torso bare except for the thin material of my bikini. Will doesn't seem to notice my discomfort, just laughs and says: 'It's one of the few things I'm good at, after all.'

The olive groves are close around us and we are quiet now, walking side by side through the green hush. I can see the wild place in the distance: blueness where the olive trees part. Will's breath rises and falls in his chest and the smell of his skin, his sweat is clean and male and wholly alive.

'This is where you went that day you disappeared,' he states as we emerge from the trees and I nod, point to the rocks down which we must climb to reach the beach.

'Yes. I was almost scared of it when I was here, but afterwards I knew I'd come back again. You go first,' I say and then regret the politeness because this place is still mine, even when shared. The wall of rock is higher and sheerer than I remember but Will's height makes it less of an effort for him than it will be for me. I hesitate, wondering how I managed this last time, whether there might be a better way, somewhere farther along the wall.

'It'll be easier if you turn round,' says Will a minute later, shading his eyes and looking up at me.

'I know.'

I turn my back to him and crouch down, stretching one leg down the rocks in search of a foothold. I find one, steady myself, and then transfer my weight on to that foot. My other seeks out a second place and in a moment or two I have made it down on to the little ledge. I crouch again, letting one leg swing back over the edge, but though my toes dig blindly at the surface of the wall, I cannot find a foothold in which to rest. I am about to give up, try another spot when cool fingers close around my skin and I feel Will guiding my foot down.

'Thanks,' I say and then keep going. I transfer my weight again, let my first foot move from its niche and this time I find a foothold without any trouble but something goes wrong when I try to let my weight rest there, the weakness in that ankle and the sound of falling rock and suddenly I am sliding, my hands, my fingernails scrabbling at the blurring surface of the rock, at air. 'Shit!' I cry and then everything stops and I am on the shingle and Will's arms are around my waist, holding me firm, steadying me.

The world is still again, quite safe, but I cannot stop myself. Silence rings in my ears as my fingers reach out, crossing the air between us, and then run over the coarse red-brown hairs on his forearms. I fit my own hands over Will's and he does not stop me and his breath is hard in my ear now, hot through my hair. Then everything is moving, his hands wrenching down my shorts, pulling aside my bikini bottoms and me helping him. He is inside me in a matter of seconds. I come almost immediately, crushing my mouth against the grainy, salty roughness of the rock face, my saliva dark and sticky on its surface, and it is too much, too painful after all this time wanting, but my hands are gripping his, making him touch me again, and Will is clutching at my breasts, his teeth in my skin, and then we are down amongst hot bruising pebbles without knowing how we got there and I am biting him, tasting the blood of him and he is whispering wild things in my ears and a voice in my head is saying: 'This is Susie's husband,' and, 'This is Will.'

But I am not listening because Will's fingers, the thickness of his tongue, the solid weight of him, are everywhere, blotting out everything. The great burning eye of the sun is above us, turning my vision red, blind, and Will does what he wants with me beneath this empty sky. I hear the roaring of the sea and the harshness of his breath, ragged in my ears, the cry of some seabird echoing from the rocks.

*   *   *

'What will we do?' I ask him, later when we have let the sea wash us clean. My body is sore and happy, bobbing on the exuberant waves that try to return us to the land, and I wish that I had not asked that question now, when I do not need to know. 'Sorry. It doesn't matter.'

'I don't know,' he says. 'I don't know.' We lie in the sun until we are dry, clamber back up the rocks and walk back up the hill in silence. We do not kiss again.

'Do you know what she says about *you*?' says Will, speaking suddenly as we reach the crest of the hill and rest for a moment.

'What?' I say, in trepidation.

'That you're the only person she's ever known who didn't want to take something of her away with them. As a kind of souvenir, she means.'

'Oh.' I stare out towards the rocky limbs of Ithaka, pondering this. 'Perhaps this is not the best time to tell me that. Anyway, I'm not sure that it's intended as a compliment. I mean, isn't that partly what a relationship is supposed to be about, giving away pieces of yourself? Trusting another person to take care of them?' I think of Joe, asleep in bed, and how we have lost that faith in one another, have built mean little walls around ourselves. 'It makes me sound ineffectual, more than anything else,' I complain. 'Not much more than a travelling companion.' Will reaches out his hand to me, links his fingers through mine.

'Cheer up, Alice.' He is smiling but there is a touch of bitterness in his voice. 'That's probably the best anyone gets from Susie.'

CHAPTER 30

'Oooh,' squeals Miranda in her little girl's voice, catching me in front of the mirror. 'You look *transformed* tonight! Doesn't she, Vee?' My mother's name is Valerie, but Miranda – who lives in the next street and is one of my mother's few long-term friends – insists on shortening it in this way. Miranda installs art wherever anyone lets her and herself at our kitchen table on an almost permanent basis. She wears jangly charm bracelets around her wrists, keeps her frizz of hair girlishly long, almost down to her waist, and talks all the time about people 'finding themselves', though surely most of us would be running away from our true selves at a rate of knots if it were humanly possible. My mother squeezes into our tiny hallway to observe me.

'What have you done to yourself, Ali?'

'Nothing,' I mutter, furious with Miranda for drawing attention to me in this way. 'It's too hot to dry my hair, that's all.'

My mother puts her head on one side, runs a hand through the loose waves of my hair and then stands back. 'You look beautiful,' she pronounces unexpectedly.

'Really?' Despite myself, I feel a flush of pleasure rising on my cheeks.

She nods. 'Are you going somewhere special?'

'Just to the Grand with the others,' I say and she reaches into her pocket and slips me a rare twenty-pound note, a prize for my unexpected beauty. To my relief, she and Miranda disappear after that, join the rest of the crowd who are already spilling from the kitchen into the yard – the beginnings of another party.

I check my appearance again in the hallway mirror. Instead of my usual uniform of black I am wearing a plain white shift dress which Susie made for me and which I have never worn until now, because without a suntan the colour seemed to make me disappear. I stand on tiptoe, craning to see the rest of me. My toenails are painted a pale gold colour and I have borrowed a pair of Hannah's sandals, with light jewelled straps that just about cover the scabs on my heels. For once, Miranda is right: I *do* look like a different person tonight. I have left off painting the usual hard black lines around my eyes and there is something open and hopeful in my expression. Apprehension too, but I dismiss it. 'What thou love'st well shall not be reft from thee.'

The Grand is a run-down hotel built of dirty red brick on the edge of town. When the guests stopped coming some ten or so years ago, the management tried to lure them back at first by refurbishing rooms and making half-hearted attempts to attract the conference crowd and then gave up and converted the building into a nightclub. Tonight is Over Eighteens' Night but nobody ever bothers to enforce the age restriction and we trip past the bouncers on the door and straight upstairs to the bar without any problem. It is so hot tonight that a pair of fire doors have been propped open and people are milling around on a concrete terrace outside. A triangle of sunlight catches one corner of the terrace. On the edges of this, girls in pale pastel clothes move, almost in slow motion, glowing like flowers in the promise of night.

I go straight to the bar, order a drink and finish it almost immediately. Then I light a cigarette and pull the smoke into the very bottom of my lungs. I am blind to what lies beyond this evening, have no visions of a relationship with Will, just a pulse beating urgently in my head. The other girls wander off, to the dance floor, out on to the terrace, catching up with school friends, but I stay where I am, needing to be alone.

I am watching him. He is talking to someone by the dance floor, a boy of about his own age whom I do not recognise, has to lean in towards him to hear what he is saying above the music. I wonder at the quiet beauty of him, filling this deafening room. He must feel my eyes on him then, for he glances over towards the bar, is about to let his eyes slip away again when he spots me among the crowd. Will smiles and it is not his usual boyish grin, quick and non-committal. There is something in it I have not seen before and music is thudding in my ears, vibrating up through the splintering floorboards into my bones, an almost unbearable excitement flaring up in the pit of my stomach. I turn away in confusion, order another drink. Though I am sober I can barely see in front of me.

I cannot wait any longer, have to act *now*, before the night is over and it is too late. My legs are moving as if they belong to someone else and then Will is here, in front of me, too quickly, as if I had sprinted across the room instead of walking as casually as I could manage. I wonder if anyone is watching us. The whole world should be watching us. He has turned away from whoever he is talking to now, blocking out their presence.

'Hi,' he says. 'You look nice.'

'I wasn't sure if you were coming tonight.' The words leave my mouth wrongly, already have a desperate edge. I feel sweat rising on my brow, trickling down the small of my back. Even with the doors open it is stifling in here.

'George gave me the night off in the end.' It's not until you are in close like this that you realise how tall he is, how his shoulders are just about to broaden. Will wipes his brow and then he smiles down at me, that same private smile he used earlier, and I am about to do it – just keep on going, straight into his arms, make everything simple. Suddenly his eyes slide away from mine. Behind him, other people lose track of conversations, start to crane their necks. I turn quickly, following their gazes, to see what they are looking at and then I don't need to ask because standing at the head of the stairs, aglow in the last shaft of sunlight from the terrace, is Susie.

She is bare-footed, carrying her shoes in one hand for some reason, and dressed quite unlike anyone else in this building, in a white 1950s' style dress with a narrow waist and a huge billowing skirt. Her black hair is even shorter than when I last saw her, chopped into a gamine crop. The dress will be one of her own creations: I can see where it strains over her small breasts, know that it will have carelessly sewn seams and badly cut wodges of material on the inside, but from here Susie's collarbone and shoulders rise up out of that dress like pale marble and she looks quite extraordinary, an unearthly vision in the midst of this crumbling hotel.

'Who is that?' says Will, not looking at me as he speaks, and in that moment, before she is even aware of his exist-ence, my best friend steals him away from me, takes the boy who was meant to be mine for herself.

CHAPTER 31

'Samuel has something to show you all,' I announce. Every-one on our little beach looks expectantly at Samuel, who is standing in the shallows with his arms wrapped across his chest.

'Come on,' he whispers to me, beckoning. 'You have to help!' I shake my head.

'You can do it,' I urge him. 'You managed without me last time.' But Samuel is emphatic and so together we wade out into deeper water and then I take up a position at a few metres' distance from him. He takes a deep breath, glances back towards the beach to ensure that everyone is paying attention, and then launches himself towards me.

For the rest of the morning I concentrate on helping Samuel to swim a little farther each time and you could almost start to believe that nothing has changed, with Susie chattering to me from the water's edge, telling me about some job with a travel company for which she's thinking of applying, and never a shadow of those minutes out on the terrace yesterday when a whole world of incomprehension came down between us.

'Come on!' I call, as Samuel's arms stir up the sea. 'Swim to me!'

And it is better this way, keeping busy, talking all the time, so that the aching between my thighs and the memory of the weight of Will upon me does not have to be arranged into any kind of order in my head. Will looks up from the book he is reading just once. We exchange the briefest of glances and yet it seems impossible to me that such an act should go unnoticed, am almost convinced that we are being observed. But Joe is fiddling around with Milly's headphones, trying to fix them for her, and Susie has her back to us, is swimming serenely over the flat surface of the water, and I realise that I am mistaken.

We eat lunch from the cool-bag Susie and Will brought down from the villa. The breeze is getting up a little and Joe is restless, says it would be a good day for sailing, then, after a minute or two of pacing along the water's edge, that he's going to dive from the rocks on the far side of the bay. I watch him as he swims out through the waves. Soon he is clambering out of the water and up on to the little overhang he must have spotted from the beach. He is well tanned by now but the bare skin on his back – which glints in the sunlight and swells slightly where it meets the top of his swimming shorts – suddenly appears vulnerable from here, as if it might tear like tissue paper, snagging on those sharp rocks. I feel a moment of fear as he stands balanced on that overhang, waiting to launch himself forwards, not because I doubt his ability but because I am imagining myself in his place, high above the water with the air pulling at him, wanting to take hold of him as if he were a feather, a playful, weightless thing, instead of something solid with a mass that the earth will always reclaim. Joe rises on his toes, lifts his arms and then, just as he launches himself into the air, he seems to falter or lose his balance, twisting slightly to one side. The swallow dive he is attempting is immediately all wrong, turning in upon itself, too close to the rocks. I see him trying to compensate, the dive losing its form altogether halfway down and Joe's legs splitting, like scissors opening and closing in the bright air, as he tries to propel himself out, away from the land. For a moment he seems to hang there, suspended above the rocks, and then he wavers again and I am already in the shallows without knowing what I am doing. Joe is swallowed up by the water and I am standing quite still. Counting seconds in my head and not moving. One, two, three, four . . . as the waves lap over my feet.

'What happened?' says Susie, coming up beside me. 'Did he slip or something?' And then: 'Oh no, he's fine,' as Joe's head breaks through the surface. Arms lifting, he starts to carve an efficient crawl back through the water towards the shore.

'You're not supposed to swim so soon after eating,' Samuel informs us. 'You might get cramp and drown.'

Back on the beach, I take a bottle of water from the cool-bag and drink. The liquid chill is a shock at the core of me and I close my eyes and concentrate on it, force myself to stop picturing the simplicity of that blank sea, the terrible allure it held for those long seconds before Joe's head emerged and made everything personal and complex again.

By mid-afternoon, Samuel has spent so long standing bare-shouldered in the glare of the sun that he has to retire to the darkness of his bedroom with a headache. One by one, as the heat of the day solidifies, the rest of us follow him up to the villa, to read or doze in the relative coolness of the living-room.

A small, unfamiliar click comes from the hallway and then the telephone rings. We all look at one another questioningly. The ring is high and tinny and it startles us like an intruder.

'Could be Alexia,' suggests Susie. Nobody moves, so in the end Will goes out into the hallway and it becomes clear that whoever is on the other end of the line is no stranger. In a second he returns.

'It's Michaelis,' he says. 'For you, sweetheart.' Milly, who has been miserable all day, waiting for a boat to arrive on our beach, leaps up from the sofa and then seems to check herself, walking carefully to the door as if she is frightened of breaking something. We can hear Milly's voice from the hallway, high and uncertain. A minute later, she flies back into the room, her eyes alight.

'Dad, Michaelis wants to know if I can go for dinner at his house tonight?'

'Just you?' says Susie, looking up from a magazine. Milly carries on looking at her father, as if it were he and not her mother who has spoken.

'Well, he said Samuel too, but I told him about the headache.' Will nods his head, thinking.

'How will you get home?' he asks. 'I wouldn't want you coming back in that boat in the dark.'

'He says his aunt and cousins from town are coming too and that they'll drop me back in their car on their way home.'

'I think that would be OK, don't you?' says Will.

For a second, I think Susie is going to disagree and then she shrugs: 'Pretty tedious with everyone speaking Greek all night.'

'I can talk to Michaelis, can't I?' says Milly, immediately beginning to rail. Her eyes seek out mine. *You see*, they say.

'He's already told us that his aunt and cousins lived in America for years,' says Will, intervening. In an even tone: 'Milly will have a nice time.'

'Well, you'd better go and tidy yourself up then, hadn't you?' says Susie, eyeing her daughter and then returning to her magazine.

The walls feel too close tonight. It is hours since I heard Milly returning from Michaelis's house. Will's voice in the driveway, thanking the aunt for bringing her home, the front door closing. I can picture the look on Milly's round face as she took herself off to bed, how she must have held her secret close to her, glowing with the purity of love. I shut my eyes, willing sleep to come, but it resists. Joe's sleeping body is oppressive beside me. I turn on my side, look at him as he sleeps, his face falling into heavier lines around his mouth, and I am full of pity for the people we have been, the meted-out love we have offered one another, held tight to ourselves as if only limited stocks were available. The night stretches out before me, begins to skew perspectives. Gradually, lying here in the dark, Joe and I are diminished to pointless creatures, scurrying aimlessly around upon the surface of the earth, and then, in the hyper-reality of semi-consciousness where my mind races in wild, overlapping circles, we grow to hideous proportions, become coarse, irredeemable caricatures of ourselves. I begin to hate us all – me and Joe, Susie and Will – find our failures and deceptions execrable, find myself believing that Susie's refusal to pretend to be anything other than self-serving is the nearest any of us comes to honesty and yet thinking this friend of mine no less despicable than the rest of us.

I sit up abruptly, deliberately breaking through the veneer of half-sleep, take a breath deep into my lungs. Quietly, I slip from the bed, pull on my dressing-gown and leave the room. In the kitchen, I wait for my eyes to adjust to the darkness and then open the fridge. It glows into the darkness, hums like a satisfied cicada.

'Hi,' says a whispered voice behind me, making me jump.

'Hi!' I do not reach for the water I have come to fetch.

'I thought it was you.'

'Yes.'

And then my dressing-gown is around my feet and Will's hands are between my legs, pushing up inside me, pushing aside all nuances, all imaginings, making way for hard reality.

'Not here,' I manage, letting go of him and trying to breathe.

'OK,' he says, and he takes me by the hand and draws me down the hallway, past the room where Joe is sleeping and out of the front door. We run across the driveway – as still and brightly lit as a stage-set – like shadow puppets, and down the steps to the pool terrace. Here the walls are blackened with night-scented shrubs, and the dark water seems to stir at our coming, ripples travelling across its surface. 'I kept thinking about you,' he says. 'I felt so bad about everything but I wanted to talk to you and . . . ' I shut him up with my mouth, my hands finding their way through his hair and right down to his scalp and my teeth drawing blood from him again, making him cry out, taking back what once was mine, or almost mine.

'You're a cruel woman . . . ' he jokes, reaching for my breasts as I push him down on to the paving and sit astride him. I take his hand and push it deep into my mouth, his fingers in the back of my throat so that I am almost gagging, and the paving-stones are rough beneath my knees, grazing my skin and this is what I have craved, one simple physical truth. Then the world changes and Will is above me, blocking out the stars, and the solid needed weight of him, the friction of his skin and his greedy mouth, taking from me, are too much. The whole night contracts inside me and then explodes and we are all that remains: a mess of semen and saliva and blood.

I bathe my knees in the bathroom without turning on the light and then slide back into bed beside Joe. Seconds later, I am asleep.

CHAPTER 32

Will and Susie become an ubiquitous sight in Daycliffe, walking its streets hand in hand, a link which both holds them together and sets them apart from everyone else, Will's solid outline the perfect foil for Susie's urban ragbag glamour. And through all of this I live vicariously, tagging along with them from time to time, gobbling up every morsel of information that Susie feeds me. Together we wonder at Will's voracious appetite – hands sliding under Susie's clothes in alleyways and shop doorways, Susie bent backwards over the bonnets of cars in darkened streets, Will ripping at her already ripped clothing – and I begin to think that there can be no end to the two of them. Susie still disappears without warning, but now everyone knows where she has gone: to Oxford, where Will pins her down like some rare butterfly on desks in dark corners of libraries, or in empty tutorial rooms, offers up her strange beauty at formal dinners and student bars and parties. Those two things, Oxford and Will, become inextricable in my mind and I question Susie endlessly after her visits, but, while she will happily share every last detail of what Will does to her when they are alone – relating this with a cool detachment more in keeping with an observer than a participant – she is frustratingly reticent on the subject of Oxford and even more so on that luminous entity which I can almost but not quite imagine: the university itself, a place which, in my mind, is populated by beings of supreme, other-worldly status, half-dreamed.

'Everyone's too friendly,' she complains, explaining why she has drawn up outside my house a day earlier than expected in the old white mini her father gave her. *'Especially* the girls.' And I understand a little of what she means because in this town we keep our distance from one another and overt attempts at friendship are considered at the very least an admission of weakness, if not downright suspicious.

*   *   *

The school year passes. I meet my classmates in a newly opened wine bar and drink cocktails, saying little though the end-of-year exams have just finished, because it is not last summer and this place is not the Waterside Inn. I am almost certain that I have done enough to ensure the school submits an excellent academic report with my college application – which names only one university – but tonight I am black with pessimism, have convinced myself that I have been deluded all this time. By my third margarita, I can see no way in which someone like me, from a town like this, could be absorbed into the rarefied fabric of Oxford, or, indeed, how Susie could ever become invisible to Will. All of this is impossible and always has been.

'Want another?' says a voice beside me.

'What?' I say. 'Why?'

'You look like you need cheering up,' smiles the man.

How morose I must look, here in this airy bar with bright chatter and laughter all around me! Embarrassment makes me defensive.

'Oh, please . . . ' I say coldly. 'Try *not* to say it might never happen, I don't think I could bear it.'

The smile fades. 'Look, don't worry about it.' His tone remains easy and he makes to move away from me. He is dark eyed and, I notice, beautiful.

'Sorry,' I say. 'I suppose I meant yes.'

Joe has been in town for one week. He is a teacher, newly qualified, has come to Daycliffe to teach at the local comprehensive, a post he will take up in September. He knows no one yet. Within weeks, he only wants to see me, to find his way inside me night after night as we hang on to one another, trying not to fall out of the narrow single bed in the flat he rents in town. Afterwards, we lie naked for hours, and Joe tries to explain his idea of maths to me, because he can see that I do not quite understand. To me, art is books and paintings and poetry, and as he speaks my mind turns back to all those years of worrying away at quadratic equations, binary numbers, Venn diagrams and logarithmic tables which I did because I needed to pass exams. But, I explain, mathematics was never a discipline that came naturally to me, like English or history or languages, that I only ever reached the minimum standard required, never had any real aptitude for the subject or any understanding of where these groupings of numbers had arrived from or, indeed, why I should be expected to trouble myself with them. Sometimes one of the class ingrates would groan theatrically – limbs splayed messily across the desk, the floor, as if they have just been dropped there from a high point – and demand to know why, exactly, we need to know all this, and some hapless teacher would talk vaguely about computers and everything in life having a mathematical explanation, but for me there was no way of knowing if they spoke the truth: these random arrangements of numbers and letters bore no relation to anything I recognised, might as well have existed in a vacuum.

But Joe wants me to understand the inherent beauty and purity of mathematics, feels sure that comprehension will dawn on me if he persists, and I do not stop him because his eyes are liquid, shining, his finely shaped hands moving all the time, framing his words as he speaks, and it is this passion in him that draws me to him, because the mundanity of this town – the acceptance of life as it comes, unleavened by hope or excitement – could find its way inside of you, could gnaw away at you, eating you from the inside out until you are a hollow person.

CHAPTER 33

There is no time for finesse or languor in our relationship, if it could be termed that. Will pushes himself inside me – fingers, tongue, cock – like a frantic boy: in the olive grove on the way to or from the beach, on the pool terrace late at night, even once in the bathroom during dinner, and each time I am ready for him, come almost instantly. One day we swim out beyond the rocks at the edge of the bay – where Joe and Susie are sunbathing, Samuel is playing at the water's edge and Milly is scribbling in her notebook – and fuck waist-high in salt-water, the black rocks which just shelter us from sight bruising my spine and Will's hand jammed across my mouth to stop my cries. We are as bad as Milly and Michaelis, worse, because we have no self-control, no quiet centre. Will's slightest glance across a room leaves me hot and wanting, squirming on my seat like an adolescent girl, alive for his touch, the weight of his body, and then I do not think about Susie or Joe or anyone else. I will go anywhere, do anything he wants, his hands pushing hard under my skirt, his mouth upon me, opening me up for himself whenever he needs to. One day he strokes my stomach when he is inside me, says what if we made a baby?

'What?' I say, the shock of it jolting through me.

'Susie told me how much you want one,' he says and then, seeing my confusion at the mention of her name when we are doing *this,* that I am about to pull away from him, he stops my mouth with his own, and after that I do not care any longer for I am awash with him, have strange, beguiling imaginings: his semen travelling around my body, entering my bloodstream, thrumming in my ears like the rush of the sea, through my heart. In the days that follow, food tastes good in my mouth, better than it ever has done before, and the heat melts me, makes me indolent and happy, my limbs replete.

'If I had a kid like Samuel,' says Joe one day in our room, while I stand naked before him, rubbing lotion into my body, which feels stronger beneath my hands today, the blood warm and close beneath my skin. 'I think it would be OK.' He waits for me to dart down upon this glittering object, like a greedy magpie, but I do not respond immediately, am busy looking at myself in the mirror. My body is firm and golden, ripe-looking from the food I have eaten. I am not old yet, I say to myself in wonder.

'Yes?' I say, seeing that Joe is still waiting for a response. I squeeze another blob of tangerine-coloured lotion from the bottle and begin working it into my stomach. I can feel the strained muscles there, where Will has been.

Joe watches me. 'It's been good these last couple of weeks. Spending a bit of time with the children.'

'With Samuel, you mean,' I correct him, and still I see he is waiting for me to say more and I will not help him. Sensing a new weakness in him, I have never felt harder, nor braver.

'Well, Milly's not really amenable to . . . She seems to have taken to you more than me . . . ' Joe gets up from the bed, comes to stand behind me so that I can see him in the mirror. 'Alice, I think I might have changed my mind!' he says, and the excitement of the gift he is about to give me begins to swell in his voice. 'We should get married. Maybe even think about starting our own family.'

I focus on myself in the mirror, narrow my eyes so that the outline of him standing behind me is blurred, could almost, if I tried hard not to notice it, not be there at all. 'That's the most selfish thing you've ever said to me, Joe.'

Susie takes little part in the idle chatter about how we should spend our last days on the island. Almost imperceptibly, a separateness seems to have gathered around her as she lies in the sun each day, with her eyes closed. When she speaks to me I am careful, watching for suspicion in her eyes, but there is none. She talks readily enough when it pleases her – about Will's work for the American computer company, how it might mean they'll have to move abroad at some point – and yet there are no more affectionate references to our schooldays, no more bringing me to account for my life.

'Ask Alice,' she says, when Samuel wants someone to come swimming or snorkelling with him.

'There,' I say to Milly, when I have finished fixing the little plaits all over her scalp. Later, when they have dried in the sun, she can run her fingers through them to loosen them into pretty waves, ready for when Michaelis comes this evening. She smiles at me in gratitude and her face is still sweet and young like this and I want to swing her round, to show her mother just how easy it is to make her daughter happy.

Lying face down next to Susie on the beach, daring to trace Will's initial in the sand beneath my sun-lounger, I try to make sense of how I feel about this friend of mine, who once took away everything I wanted. The hot immediacy of Will marks my body like invisible bruising, almost wipes out any trace of rationality, but I am trying my best, lying here beside his wife, to examine myself.

Our friendship, I come to see, has been an odd, persistent thing, a bag full of openness and secrets, always carried. I think about Susie's power to draw others to her, to keep them there, and wonder how much happiness this has brought her, whether it is a blessing or a curse. I cannot dissemble, even to myself: Susie has hardly cared for her capacity to enthral others, might have given up Will to me in an instant had I asked her to back then. In the heat of the day I slide into fantasy because it is easier, imagine the shadow of Will cast over me always and somewhere in the middle distance behind him, Samuel and Milly, reaching out to me, blotting out Joe, blotting out . . . the past, and I have to pull myself up short because it is too captivating an image.

I swim, immerse myself in the cool silken water of the bay, try to justify what I have done by reminding myself that this family of Susie's, of Will's, which only days ago seemed gilded, is so damaged from within that it can hardly hold itself together, with or without my influence. I would be no more than a catalyst then, speeding up an inevitable process of disintegration . . . And the more I think of it, the more I come to believe that this ephemeral friendship with me is the extent of Susie's capacity to care for another human being, that she cannot connect in other ways. Looking down through the water at my newly strengthened body, my taut, brown limbs, and then up at the high blue sky, I think that here, like Samuel, I have found my true element. Then I lie right back and let the cold water find its way down to my scalp, my hair wavering on unseen currents.

CHAPTER 34

Alexia, the maid, says the weather will break next week, after we are gone, but it is hard to imagine this. For now it holds us, like insects in syrupy resin, faintly moving. Milly and Michaelis grow quieter as our last days slide past, no longer giggling together or clowning about with Samuel in the water, but taking themselves off across the bay in the boat, or to the rocks at the far end of our little cove, where they sit, facing one another, saying little. When Michaelis has to leave, Milly disappears into her bedroom, the pain of another, greater, parting beginning in her eyes. We try to make light of it, but all of us are affected by this heightened atmosphere, the gazes held too long between the two of them until the rest of us are nothing.

Again and again Will says we will be OK, though he cannot tell me how and I do not ask. He fills my ears with these words, lodges them there with the same assurance with which he does everything else, saying Susie has never loved him enough, never wanted the same things or appreciated how hard it had been for him, trying to put right the mess they made of things when they were starting out. And I do not ask what about Milly and Samuel, because I do not want all of this taken away from me before I have had the chance to walk around it, to wonder at it, leave it to Will to convince himself, telling me how it will be better for the children if the truth of this marriage were finally acknowledged. And then, after a while, the enormity of what he is contemplating becomes too much for him and he will change direction a little, saying that more than anything he cannot forgive Susie's recent callousness towards their daughter, cannot find a way to go on in the aftermath of such blatant cruelty. I should persuade him that what he is proposing is merely cruelty in another form, should stop him right there, but I never do. For the image of myself replacing Susie at the centre of that family is too beguiling.

In the middle of the night I come awake in fright. Joe is staring down at me, eyes black in the darkness, a great moon, heavy with itself, filling the window behind his head.

'What?' I gasp.

'Do you still love me?'

'What are you talking about?' I blink though I have never been more awake; pretend to strain to see the hands of my watch, green slivers glowing in the dark.

'I'm not stupid, Alice.'

'I don't know what . . . '

'I need to know.' His voice is flat, a relentless probe for the truth, but his body is fragile, bent in protectively upon itself in the moonlight, and it takes only a second for me to quell the urge to take advantage of the thing that Joe already understands: that the balance of power between us has silently altered.

'I don't know,' I say nervously. My words ring out, loud in this room that suddenly seems too confining. I am fearful, would like to gather them in again. I have not thought this through; have not *begun* to think about what will happen to Joe and me. It is too late now.

'Thanks for not lying,' says Joe in a quiet voice. And we stay like this, Joe sitting with his elbows on his knees and me lying quite still beside him, breathing in and out as calmly as I can. And I have not been brutal but I will not go to him either, will not pretend that we can change what has passed. I am beginning to think that we will stay like this all night, sleepless, but then I open my eyes and know that time has moved on for Joe is at the window, smoking a cigarette, and dawn is brightening the sky. I watch him for a minute, pull the sheet around me to protect myself from the sudden chill of morning air mingling with the sharp smell of smoke, cold in my nostrils. When I awake next, a solid column of sunlight crosses the corner of the bed, a hot white triangle, and he is gone.

CHAPTER 35

'All I know is this,' I'd say to Milly someday to make her understand that I was not party to any appointment noted in Susie's diary back then.

It is the beginning of October. Leaves cling to the trees, but today winter is in the air. All day long a persistent drizzle has been falling from skies as grey as old soap and as I walk from the bus stop towards the centre of Daycliffe, a malicious wind throws handfuls of stinging rain into my face. I pull my trench coat – purchased from a charity shop the week before – more tightly around me, turn up the tired collar in an attempt to stop the rain from seeping down my neck. The afternoon light is already beginning to fade. I pass beneath a shop canopy and the military-style buttons on my coat gleam dully, catching the glow from the brightly lit window which transforms the trays of cheap jewellery, carriage clocks and silver ornaments into something precious and magical, adrift and beckoning in the half-light. A bus thunders past, murky with people. I step aside to avoid the arc of spray from its wheels – straight into a puddle. Water finds its way through the toe of one of my boots, a growing cold, and I hurry on to the café on the High Street where Susie and Will are waiting for me. They have come to tell me they are leaving.

'But why?' I ask again, shaking my head because their words will not settle into any kind of natural order in my brain. And they tell me, once more, that it is better this way, that

Will's parents have a bigger house and more money to spare than Susie's, that it will be easier for Will to travel between London and Oxford at weekends (for everyone agrees that he must complete his degree).

'But what about you?' I demand of Susie, uninhibited, for once, by Will's presence. 'What will you *do*?'

'Look after a baby, I suppose,' says Susie. Her expression is impenetrable, her tone, reasoned. She glances down at her stomach, which has only just recently begun to swell, pushing itself out into a small, firm hillock.

'But . . . ' I am like a child myself, badgering for something it knows it cannot have, wanting to grab this Susie that I hardly recognise and shake her back to life, back to here, not that place behind her eyes where I cannot reach. 'Don't you want to be at home? Near to your mum? Your family?' *Me*, near to me, I am thinking, because from the moment I received that crowing little phonecall from a classmate, telling me the news, I have had everything worked out in my mind, seen Susie on the outside of this child again – for I am unable truly to believe in a Susie grown lumpen and clumsy – and Will a vague figure in the background, and it will be just the two of us, me and Susie, managing all this, making it right, as though it is merely another one of our secrets that we like to hold close, away from the eyes of others. Susie sighs, her eyes drawn to the café window where the rain hits the glass in long voluptuous splatters. Outside, in the coming gloom, car headlights are being switched on.

'No,' she says. 'I don't think I could stand it, Al. It was better in the beginning, when everyone was going apeshit. I could deal with that. But now everyone's fussing around me, wanting to take care of me. Do you know,' Susie gives a shudder, 'some friend of my mum's – some woman I hardly know – stopped me in the street the other day and wanted to *feel* it!' Her hands hover over her bump, demonstrating. 'Can you imagine?' Her voice rises in indignation, making the people on the next table turn to stare, and for an instant she is the girl I know again, shaking her head violently, refusing absolutely the unwelcome memory. 'Anyway, college is out the window now, for me at least,' she continues more quietly, 'and it's crowded enough in our house as it is. At least in London I'll be anonymous, not some kind of local oddity for everyone to prod at.'

'Hardly anonymous,' says Will. He has said little during this interview, just sat beside Susie, his hand covering hers. 'Mum and dad will take care of you when I'm at college and my sisters are close by.'

'I've told you, I don't want to be taken care of,' says Susie, removing her hand from beneath his, but smiling in her new, serene way. 'Oh, don't look like that, Alice! Nobody's dead, you know.'

'Sorry,' I say, pushing aside my grief, the truth of this. I make a conscious effort to remove the woebegone expression from my face. 'I'm just shocked, that's all. I thought . . . ' I try to think of something to say. 'I suppose you'll meet other mums?' I hazard.

'What?' says Susie, distracted for a second by someone she knows passing the window, raising a hand to her. 'I suppose so.' But she looks startled by the suggestion, as if the idea of meeting other mothers, of being one herself, has never occurred to her until now. We finish our coffee and then Will looks at his watch and comes round to my side of the table, gives me a hug and says something about coming to visit them both as soon as I can. The hug doesn't touch me and when he goes to the counter to settle the bill I forget to offer to pay for my coffee. I stare at Susie, thinking about all the evenings this summer when she has arrived on my doorstep, no longer distracted by sex or college or disappearing acts, just wanting to lie on her side on my bed and stare out of the window, at the sky, at the black backs of the terraces in the next street, listening to music or talking about things we used to do: schooldays, boys we thought we loved once. I guessed then – though I could not tell Milly this part, even now, when she knows the worst – that things were bad for Susie: sometimes I thought she could not bear to be alone with the evidence of her body and sometimes I believed just the opposite, that she came here to escape everyone else, to find a space for herself – but right from the start she was adamant that she did not want to talk about it, what would happen next, and I tried to do as she asked, tried not to watch her stomach, her eyes, for signs of a new life within her, and instead we laughed a lot, even more than we did before because it is hard not to think the world crazy when your best friend has something growing inside her that cannot be stopped.

'What about you, Ali? What will you do?' asks Susie. She is watching me closely across the table. The rain is falling faster outside, accelerating towards some unguessed conclusion.

'I don't know,' I say, unable to hide my despair. 'I wish you weren't going, Suse. Do you have to?'

'What about university?' asks Susie, ignoring my plea. Though her manner is direct enough, the enquiry is, by necessity, vague because until now she has not questioned me in detail about my plans for the future. I, of course, have never confided in her about Oxford, the application form on my desk at home which may or may not be sent.

I glance over my shoulder towards Will, who is still waiting in line at the counter. 'I'm not sure.' I give a little shrug, having no energy for this conversation right now. 'There's Joe now.'

'What's that got to do with anything?' flashes Susie.

'But . . . I thought you liked him?'

'Oh, Alice!' Then: 'Look, I can't do *everything* for you. Not any more.'

'What do you mean?' I say, tears starting in my eyes so that the café is a bright swimming blur.

I turn to see Will approaching, pushing change into his pocket. Susie gets up and I notice that she can no longer spring to her feet, has to ease herself out from the table before coming round to me. Her face is serene again. 'I have to go now. Will's parents are coming to collect us tomorrow and I haven't even begun to pack.' She stands back and smiles encouragingly at me. I say another quick goodbye to Will and mutter something banal about taking care of Susie and working hard. And then Susie does something she has never done before: suddenly she swoops in upon me and plants a kiss, fierce and a little clumsy, upon my cheek. For a second her belly is as hard as stone against mine and then she releases me hurriedly and we are apart again.

I stare at her, shocked by that moment of physical proximity, my hand rising automatically to my reddening cheek. 'That means you're going for good doesn't it?' I say slowly and then fresh grief breaks over me, as if I hadn't quite believed it before.

Susie says nothing, just makes a little waving gesture with her hand and looks at Will. Then they turn to go. 'By the way,' she says over her shoulder as she heads towards the door, 'I won't need the mini in London so I'm leaving it for you. Think of it as your getaway vehicle.'

I stay where I am, my empty coffee cup in front of me, watch them walking along the High Street, try to imagine Susie's tiny bedroom with all her possessions in a pile, but other than her rag-bag clothes and the little sewing machine that used to sit on her chest of drawers I cannot for the life of me think of anything she owns. For a minute or two I see their figures illuminated intermittently by the headlights of passing cars but then they are gone, swallowed up by the dark and the thickening rain.

CHAPTER 36

Michaelis arrives early, while we are still eating breakfast out on the terrace. The following day, his parents and younger brother will finally arrive from America. He says he must leave tomorrow, to travel with his grandmother into town and then on to the airport to collect them. The day after that – our last full day on the island – they will drive to the capital for his cousin's wedding. Milly, whose hair I have fixed into plaits again, hardly touches her breakfast before melting away with him, down through the olive grove to the beach, Samuel tagging along behind the two of them.

'Anyone want more coffee?' says Joe, stretching in his seat and picking up the empty cafetière. He is determinedly cheery this morning, arriving at the breakfast table wet from a morning swim instead of emerging half-asleep from our bedroom. Before anyone has a chance to answer, Dimitri arrives, driving a shiny green Land Rover and followed by another man on a motorbike. The Land Rover is for us, he says, because the other car isn't yet fixed and we will need to drive to the airport in a few days' time. All of us stand outside the Villa Stamatia and wave goodbye as Dimitri and his friend head off down the track on the motorbike.

'Come inside a moment,' says Joe, motioning to me.

'I love you,' he says. 'I don't want to lose you.'

'Oh Joe,' I say eventually, 'I don't know how I . . . '

'I told you last night,' he interrupts. 'I'm not stupid and you're not very adept at hiding things.'

'What?' My breath is shallow in my chest.

'The swimming with Samuel. Helping Milly do her hair

and everything. I'm well aware that you've been trying to prove to me how delightful family life could be, Al, and I have to admit that I was all set to resist. I felt as though you were trying to . . . to . . . con me in some way.'

'I *like* the children.'

'Look, I know you've started to give up on me,' he continues, 'but something's happened to me here, Alice – I don't know whether it was just getting away from work or something about this place,' he gestures vaguely around him. 'The way it makes everything appear simpler – but I started to get it, and last night, when I thought about losing you, what that would mean to me, I realised that you were absolutely right. I *have* been selfish.' He comes over to the bed where I am sitting and drops down, squatting in front of me. I let his words sink in, try my best to conjure up that familiar, secret image: a child with black hair and Joe's dark, searching eyes, but: *I was all set to resist.*

'I don't know . . . ' I say again, looking past him, out of the window towards Ithaka, which, though it is still early morning, is melting into a haze.

'Don't make up your mind yet,' says Joe, seizing my hands. 'We could take the car in the morning and drive somewhere for lunch, just the two of us, find a beach – '

'Will said something about needing to see Dimitri at the office,' I interrupt. It is a lie. I do not know why I have said it, except in panic.

'Well the day after then – he and Susie won't want it on the last day. He looks up at me. 'Give me a chance, Alice.' There is silence for a minute. Joe does not let my hands drop. 'These last few years haven't always been great times . . . '

'Can they ever be?' I interrupt. 'Are we capable of anything more than this?' The words hang there, a stark picture of the two of us, Joe and me.

'I don't know,' he says. 'But you have to let me try.'

*   *   *

Will and I take too many risks now. We stop the new Land Rover half way down the track, leaving the villa on the pretext of needing more food from the supermarket, and then fuck like teenagers on the back seat, clumsy limbed and both of us gasping for air, running with sweat as the sun beats down on hot metal and glinting glass and outside the cicadas screaming in fury in the undergrowth.

'We have to decide what to do,' he says. We are on the way back home – two cases of beer and a small bag of shopping on the back seat. I am leaning out of the window, smoking a cigarette from a pack of Susie's that Will was carrying in his back pocket, slightly flattened now. The insides of my thighs ache. Each time I lift my hand to my mouth, I can smell him on my skin.

'We seem to be managing well enough,' I say. Hot air reaches inside the car, tugs at my hair. We drive on and Will keeps on talking, but I am dreamy, hardly listening, because something in me still doesn't quite believe in all of Will's urgency. Then I wake up, realise that he is trying to explain something to me, making me think when I do not want to think.

' . . . Susie says that you've been hiding away from the world all this time,' he is saying.

'What?' I say, sitting up.

'She says you've started to petrify, all those years stuck in Daycliffe with Joe.'

'It's not Joe's fault,' I say, as we turn off the main road and on to the track that leads to the villa. Instinctively I feel the need to defend Joe, even now. 'It's not been easy for him either, you know.' Will raises his eyebrows, but says nothing. 'He was so grateful to get another job when the teaching went wrong, but after a while he began to loathe that too. He feels as though he's made a wrong turn somewhere in his life – with me, too, I suspect – and that he can't go back without admitting he's made mistakes.'

'Isn't that making rather heavy weather of it all?' says Will lightly, changing gear and swerving to avoid a pot-hole. 'We all make false starts along the way but they're hardly indelible.'

'To Joe, they are,' I say. 'They accumulate.' My breath comes in a heavy sigh. 'It takes a certain kind of bravery . . . Anyway, it's not as bad as all that.' My head is starting to hurt with the weight of loyalties engrained within me. I wonder what I am thinking of, imagining that I can shrug off all these years of complex, unspoken compromises between Joe and me, again aware of the knot of under-standing and resentments and dependency that holds us together.

Only as we are pulling on to the driveway of the Villa Stamatia does he remove his hand from my thigh.

'We have to think about what we're going to do,' insists Will, and I say yes, we must, but still his voice in my head: *Susie says, Susie says.*

*   *   *

Milly and Michaelis have gone down to sit on the pool terrace, seeking out cooler air and a little peace, and Samuel is in bed, tired out from the exertion of swimming all day long. It is too hot to eat properly, so between jugs of cocktails, we pick at the houmous and bread and tzatziki that Will and I brought home from the supermarket. Susie complains of a headache but she is at her most brilliant tonight, talking and drinking rapidly and hardly remembering to eat. The rest of us drink less obtrusively but nevertheless with a steady determination, Will becoming less brittle with Susie than he has been these last few days, laughing at her animation, while Joe looks young and chastened, sitting closer to me than is necessary or comfortable in this heat. Beneath the table he reaches for my hand and I take it in mine, squeeze it comfortingly.

'Michaelis has come to say good-night,' says Milly, a few hours later. 'He might be able to come for a little while tomorrow,' she explains, 'in the evening, but it'll be pretty busy once his folks arrive, so . . . ' Everyone smiles at the Americanism, so readily adopted. Milly's voice is valiant, determined to hide a slight quaver. All of us know that other relatives – from across the island and from Athens – are also arriving on the island tomorrow and that this is where our goodbyes begin. There are hugs and hand-shakings all round and Michaelis, with his customary impeccable manners, thanks us all for taking such good care of him, says he's sure we'll all meet again. A minute later he and Milly appear on the driveway beneath us and we turn away then, talk among ourselves as the two of them cross the gravel and hover where the pathway through the olive trees begins, wrapped together in semi-darkness.

'With any luck she'll go straight to bed and feel better by the morning,' observes Susie, when, eventually, we hear footsteps on the gravel again, the front door opening and closing. But a moment later Milly appears, hovering uncertainly in the doorway behind us. She has clipped back her fringe tonight and had me pull the rest of her hair into a stubby ponytail at the back of her neck and she looks younger and prettier like this, her skin lightly tanned and almost free of make-up and fine black wisps of hair softening her face. Once again, I catch a glimpse of Susie – in the shape of her mouth and the faint shadow of her cheekbones – but her eyes are her father's, round and candid and – tonight – dark with pain. And I understand that Milly *cannot* go to her room just now. She is a child, caught on the spikes of adult grief, and she is here as a child, wanting us to free her, expecting us to know how this might be done. No one says anything immediately but I pat the empty seat beside me, motion to it, and as Milly passes her father's chair, he lays a hand on her shoulder.

'OK, darling,' he says. Not a question, but an assertion or, at least, some kind of promise.

'Do you think he'll be able to come tomorrow?' says Milly in a strangled voice. There is silence for a moment: we know as much as she does.

'We hope so,' I say and Will and Joe nod their heads in a reassuring fashion. Susie rattles the ice in her empty glass.

'Oh, Milly!' she sighs, after a moment's pause. 'He probably comes whizzing over here in that little boat of his every time he spots a new bikini on the beach.' Milly's face freezes for a second. Her hand reaches for the back of the chair, for support, and then disbelief – rage – start to work themselves over her features in gradations. She opens her mouth to speak, and then she crumples, collapsing into the seat beside me as if she has been flung there by some unseen force.

'For fuck's sake, Susie!' Will has slammed his fist on to the table, is on his feet, face to face with his wife. The cocktail jug shudders and then falls on its side, begins to roll towards the edge of the table. Joe's hand flies out to save it but it falls before he can reach it, shatters. Will and Susie are staring at each other, eyes locked, bodies taut. From her chair, Milly sobs like a child, in great, mucusy gulps.

I go to her, wrap my arms around her. 'Come indoors,' I say quietly, trying to draw her up from her chair.

Will has Susie by the arm. 'Look at her!' he orders, jerking his wife forwards across the terrace, forcing her towards their weeping daughter, but though Susie does not resist, she will not look, keeps staring straight ahead of her, out across the terrace, her face set. 'Look what you've done!' bellows Will. Milly gives a convulsive sob and breaks away from me, running between her parents and inside the villa. We hear the slamming of a door from within and Susie's fingers are working furiously against the fine material of her kaftan. There is outrage in Will's eyes. He is about to say something more but then his mouth hardens and he turns and follows his daughter indoors.

Susie does not move. One of her feet is bleeding, from the broken cocktail jug, but she does not seem to notice, just stares blindly ahead of her, out into the blackness of the night, her fingers still working. Joe and I look at her, look at each other. I shake my head at him and then, without another word, we pick our way across the broken glass, and slip away inside.

An hour passes. Will taps lightly on our door.

'Milly's almost asleep now,' he says, as soon as I open it. 'She wants you though.'

'Oh.'

He waits in the doorway, looking as though he's about to say something more, but then weariness seems to overcome him. 'I'll see you in the morning,' he says.

Milly has the sheet pulled up to her chin. She is calm now, though pale. I sit beside her, reach a hand out to smooth her fringe back from her face. Her skull feels young and perfect beneath my hand.

'If Daycliffe is so awful,' she says, 'why do you still live there?'

'Lots of reasons,' I say wearily. 'Anyway, it's not important,' I add.

She closes her eyes and smiles. A minute later she is asleep.

CHAPTER 37

Susie's white mini sits outside our house all that winter, turning brown in the dirty rain. It stays there even when Milly is born just before Christmas, two weeks earlier than expected, though I keep on assuring Susie that I will visit just as soon as I can. My mother wonders why I went to the trouble of working in the library for the whole of the summer holidays to pay for driving lessons if I am not going to bother to make use of them, but in these months since Susie and Will left I have found myself merely going through the motions, hardly finding a reason to get out of bed some days, when the skies are grey and oppressive and rain falls constantly until that sound rattling against your window could drive you mad. The rain finds its way into my dreams all through a wet springtime, making everything sodden and worthless, and then one day I wake up and it is a Saturday in early summer and the sun is high in the sky, the dew is rising from the rooftops, and the world is large and waiting. Joe is away on a residential course but I will not stay at home waiting for him to return. I dress quickly, go downstairs before my mother or Hannah have awoken, and slip outside into the wet morning air.

The driver's door is stiff from lack of use and the engine does not want to start at first, but I press my foot down on the accelerator – careful not to flood the engine – and after a couple of attempts it jumps into life. I drive Susie's mini through the still empty streets to the nearest garage where I fill it with petrol, buy a road map, and then work out how to use the car wash. Five minutes later, the little car is not quite sparkling, but as close as it's ever going to be and soap residue makes a rainbow of the windscreen. It is only as I am about to drive away from the garage that I realise that I've forgotten to leave a note at home. No one will be too concerned by my absence, I think, and I am on the point of driving on, but some instinct makes me turn the other way, back towards the house. It will only add a matter of minutes to my journey, can make no difference to this day for anyone, I remind myself, not Susie or Will or Joe, cannot stop Oxford from being there at the end of this journey, waiting for me. Last year's application form is still sitting in the drawer at home, uncompleted, its blank pages waiting to be filled. I wind down the window, let the morning air chill my hands and face and wonder why it has taken me all this time to understand this simple fact. There are no leafy avenues or lush pockets of parkland here, but I can hear birdsong above the noise of the engine, coming from somewhere above these empty streets, and it is so fresh and brave that suddenly I understand how young I am and it is a good and wonderful thing. I return to the house, run inside and hurriedly scribble a note. Just as I am propping it up on the kitchen table, the phone rings in the hallway, startling me. There is movement upstairs, the creaking of a bed from my mother's room.

Back in the car, I check my map again, tracing the major roads I will have to negotiate, and then set off. Soon I am leaving behind the terraced streets and taking a short cut across the large council estate on the edge of town, which turns out not to be a short cut at all, on account of all the speed bumps along the roads here, but still it is better than having to wait at all the sets of traffic lights on the ring road. I glance in the rear-view mirror and am startled to find a van driving behind me: I had not been aware of another vehicle waiting to turn on to this road. The van is travelling close to my tail and I speed up a little, aware that a novice driver like myself might prove an irritant to someone in a hurry, on their way to work perhaps. A minute later, I check again and the van is still there, filling my rear-view mirror. I can see a man at the wheel, young and muscular, in a short-sleeved blue T-shirt.

'Go *away*,' I mutter under my breath.

My anxiety to be away from him makes me accelerate too violently and the little car judders over a large speed bump, meeting the ground on the other side more violently than I'd expected, with the grind of metal. I slow down for a second and then accelerate again, trying to open up more distance, hoping that the van might turn off into a side road and leave me in peace. I glance into the rear-view mirror, checking once more, and then back again, accelerating as I do so.

Somehow, the car is no longer moving. The van, too, has stopped. I sense people coming from behind closed doors into that empty street and somewhere the vibration of feet running along paving that is cracked from the heat of summer, yawning open. A small boy with red hair is lying face down in the road with his bicycle beside him, its front wheel still spinning. I cannot hear a thing.

'Was he *dead*?' In my mind I can hear Milly's horrified tones when I tell her the story – for I want to tell as much as I can.

'No, just cut and bruised,' I'll say, picturing that small body in the road, and for a second my ribs will feel as though they are contracting, stopping my breathing. 'It seems he'd slipped out of the house before his mother was even out of bed, set out on a little adventure of his own. Anyway, I didn't get to Oxford that day, as you can imagine.'

'Oh,' she'll say, looking disappointed, and I will smile at her and say: 'I told you it wasn't the most thrilling of tales,' and she will never know – will never need to know – that I have only told her half of the story, that the person who answered that ringing phone in the hallway was not my mother, but me, and that Oxford was no longer in my thoughts when I left the house and set out for the second time that morning.

CHAPTER 38

I leave Milly's room, closing the door quietly behind me, and then go into the kitchen, needing some water.

'Alice!' A low voice from the terrace. In the darkness, I see her, still standing among the broken glass and there is no pity in my soul.

'What do you want?' and Susie walks towards me, soft skin over glittering shards, unnoticed.

'Is she OK?'

'She'll be fine,' I say in my most self-contained voice. 'She's asleep.'

'That's good.' Susie glances towards her own bedroom. 'I think Will must be too.' She keeps coming towards me and I starting to think that there is madness in that smile, madness out there on that terrace, when she says: 'I think he's ready now.'

'What for?'

'To let me go.'

'He's spoken to you?' I say at last.

Susie smiles, wryly this time. 'No, but tonight ought to do it, don't you think?'

'I meant . . . ' I am struggling with this. The consequences, the implications. 'How do you know?'

'I've always known.'

'What?' I snap. Panic – for somehow I have never imagined this moment. She sits down on one of the sofas, motions to me to do the same. I stay where I am, trying to contain the shaking that starts in my stomach and wants to take over my limbs.

'I knew you were in love with him years ago.'

'No.'

'It was obvious, Al. The way you'd lap up everything I told you about him and then suddenly looked so . . . *crushed* by it. I must admit it took me a while to work it out though. You see, if I'd known sooner you could have had him, but by the time I'd realised, it was too late. Will was stuck to me like a leech.'

'Don't you love him?' I say in wonder, shaken by the contrast between her serene expression and the brutality of her words. Susie reaches for a packet of cigarettes on the coffee table and lights one before answering.

'I'm not sure,' she says, pushing the packet towards me. 'Maybe.' I ignore her offering. 'What it comes down to, I suppose, is that I'm not a very nice person, even when it comes to my own children.'

I think of Milly's words in the kitchen, the first time she approached me, asking me what I thought of her mother.

'Do you want them?' Susie asks simply. And her expression is tranquil and enquiring.

'Don't be so . . . ' Slowly, surely, other words rise to the surface in my mind, gather momentum until they are rushing in upon me, wanting attention, each of them bringing new meanings with them. Susie sending me off with her husband, insisting to Joe: 'But your arm's a real mess.' 'I'm not sure you'd manage to ride all the way back.' Will whispering about babies into my ear: 'Susie told me.' And Susie herself, telling her own children: 'Ask Alice,' 'Go to Alice.' I throw down the packet of cigarettes. 'What kind of a question is that?!'

'Not so outrageous, Al,' she counters. 'You're sleeping with my husband.' This fact, bald and inescapable, silences me. 'I'm giving you what you want,' says Susie in a friendly kind of voice. Then she stands up, stretches her arms above her head and yawns. 'I should sleep now.' I say nothing, refuse to meet her eye. 'Well,' she says and turns to go. Over her shoulder she adds. 'Don't leave it too long though, Al,' the first note of anxiety tightening her voice. 'Will won't stay angry with me for ever.'

CHAPTER 39

'Come and get me,' said Susie.

'What?' The line is crackling and I can hear traffic noise in the background, lorries bearing down. 'Where are you?'

'In a phone box.'

'Yes but *where*? Why aren't you ringing from home?'

'I can't stand it any more. I have to get away from here.' Her voice is flat, determined.

'But . . . what about Will? Have you had a fight or something? Have you talked to him?'

'What would I say?'

'OK,' I reply, thinking that this is something to be discussed later. 'But how about Milly? How will we manage?' I picture the phone box, wonder how Susie is coping with the pushchair, whether she has had to prop open the door with it, which would account for the traffic noise in the background, or whether she has left it outside and has the baby in her arms. I have a vague idea that we might need a car seat for Milly, wonder whether Susie has one already or whether we will have to buy one from somewhere. Then something bad begins to form in my mind. 'You'll need to go back to fetch her things, won't you?' The statement becomes a question, betraying my concern. Silence. Down the line I can hear the phone box vibrating as more traffic whooshes past. Eventually: 'She's at home. With Will's mother. You have to rescue me, Alice.' And she says I'm not to ask her anything more, just come, and I find myself saying yes, of course I will, and it is only late that evening – after the confusion and shock of the accident – that I try to reach her, telephoning Will's parents because I cannot think of anything else to do.

'Have you heard from Susie? Has she come back yet?' I ask breathlessly.

'Yes,' says Will's mother, clearly puzzled by the urgency of my tone. 'I'll just fetch her for you.' She returns to the phone a minute later, tells me that Susie is busy bathing Milly and that she'll call me some time tomorrow, or perhaps the day after that.

CHAPTER 40

Joe stirs beside me though it is still early. I slide out of bed as quietly as possible, dress in the bathroom and then slip out of the room before he wakes. Stepping out of the front door, I feel an immediate sense of release. The sky is high and blue above me, and the light still lemony, tinged with green above the olive groves. Soon the heat of the day will bleach all colour from it. I stand for a second and blink, allowing my eyes to adjust. Out here, in this vast bowl of light and rock and sea, everything should seem smaller, simpler. Out here it will be easier to know what should happen next.

I make my way down through the trees, eschewing the path that leads off to my left, towards Michaelis's house and on to the wild place, and continuing towards our own little beach. Today I need to think clearly, not allow myself to be distracted by the whispering of the olive groves and fanciful notions of other worlds held within them, just missed: the scattering of hooves, of bare feet, as I approach. I step out of the trees on to that narrow, rocky path, high above the bay, and see Susie, standing on the path directly beneath me, where it switches back on itself. She looks up and waves, waits for me to join her.

'I thought you might come down here,' she says, when I reach her. 'I don't know why.'

'I didn't sleep very well.'

'No.' It is almost impossible to meet her eye this morning, knowing what she knows. She seems to register my discomfort because she turns away from me, leans on the little stone wall and looks out across the bay as though admiring the view for the first time. One of the stones shifts under the weight of her elbow and a little shower of pale sand trickles down the wall.

'Careful,' I say, but it is a gentle warning and my voice is even.

'You're not scared any more,' pronounces Susie, turning to look at me.

'It's not so far down from here,' I say, but she is right and I had not known it till now. I wait a moment more: 'Look, what about Samuel and Milly? What's going to happen to them in all this?'

Susie's gaze is steady. 'That's up to you now, isn't it?'

'*I'm* not their mother!' I hiss, last night's fury flaring up unexpectedly. I breathe deeply. 'Don't you love them at all?'

'Yes, but it's the wrong question, Alice,' she says, with a shake of her head. 'The right question is: Should I have let them love me?' I do not reply to this. I see now that there is nothing to be gained by accusations of selfishness or cruelty, all the things that passed through my mind in the long hours before dawn. I would only be confronting Susie with what she already knows.

I push air out of my lungs, cross the path and stand beside her.

'Can I have a cigarette?' seeing the packet in her hand. I lean against the wall beside her and both of us light up. Another stone shifts, another trickle of sand.

'Do you think we could jump from here?' says Susie, leaning out farther. I follow her gaze, down the hillside below us, think that you might just survive the drop to the beach if it were vertical, but the ground falls away in fits and starts, great chunks of protruding rock waiting to shatter bones, thorny shrubs to hold flesh like scraps in the wind. It is the studied casualness of Susie's tone that frightens me.

'No,' I say carefully, 'I don't.'

She swings round to me abruptly, startling me, her eyes wild. 'What else then?' she demands. 'What else?!'

I breathe slowly. 'We could just turn back the way we came.'

'But I could do this *now*, with you here!' she says, her voice rising. 'Couldn't you, Al?' She seizes my arm. 'Just imagine if we made it! And if we didn't . . . ' I think of that day on the mountain, Susie riding the scooter as though the world was collapsing in upon itself behind us, and for the first time I see that for some reason I can't quite fathom, except that it is to do with our shared past, our youth, my presence in her life has come to be a signifier of liberty, of an ability to choose. I say nothing for a moment.

'The others will be up by now,' I remind her.

'Yes.' Susie drops my arm, grinds out her cigarette on the wall and then moves back into the middle of the path. Suddenly, she grins: 'It was a ridiculous idea anyway.'

In the pool, Samuel leaves off dive-bombing Milly to call to his mother. 'Can't we go to the beach?'

'Not today,' says Susie from her sun-lounger.

'Why not?'

'Because everyone's happy here.'

'I'm not,' pronounces Samuel. 'I need to swim.' Susie lifts her sunglasses, gives him a look of incomprehension and gestures towards the pool. 'No, I mean *properly* swim,' he explains.

'Why don't you do some lengths?' asks Will, coming to the edge of the water. 'I'll count them for you.'

Samuel shakes his head. 'What's the point in swimming up and down the same old bit of water? There's nothing new to see.'

'I could teach you to dive,' offers Will.

'No thanks, dad,' says Samuel, looking apologetic.

Will swims up to me.

'Can you get away early in the morning?' he asks in a low

voice. 'We could go to our beach and be back before anyone else is up.'

'I don't know,' I say, thinking of Joe's plans for our last day on the island. 'I could try but I'm worried that Joe will start to suspect something.'

Will glances across at him, asleep on a sun-lounger. 'Well, he's barely conscious most of the time.' He smiles, waits for me to smile back.

'What would *you* know about anything?' I say angrily and I turn and swim away in fast little strokes to the other side of the pool. He dives beneath the water and comes up beside me a second later.

'Sorry,' he whispers, taking my hand beneath the water. 'I didn't mean to upset you. It's just we're running out of time and we need to decide how this is going to happen.' I nod, smile at him and let it pass, but later, lying in the sun, the smugness of Will's observation, his belief that my loyalties are firmly fixed with him now, still rankles. I want to go to him right away, snatch that book out of his hands and tell him Susie may be looking in the other direction right now but that she knows everything, has always known, see that smile fall to pieces on his face.

CHAPTER 41

The heat of the day lies in wait outside the half-open shutters of our bedroom. I glance at my watch. It is still siesta time. There is still time to think, to decide, to arrive at a solution. Joe sleeps on, untroubled by the changing world around him. He is like a child. I think back to this morning, Susie hovering on the edge of that cliff, consumed, for a moment, with excitement, and then that slow, companionable walk back up to the villa, as if something had been settled when in reality nothing had been resolved. As we came in sight of the villa she smiled at me, looked almost happy.

'We'll be OK,' she said, linking an arm through mine.

I lie still, try to concentrate on what has happened here, what should happen to bring it towards some kind of conclusion, but what keeps coming back to me, like some kind of revelation constantly opening up before me, blocking out everything else that I must arrange into some kind of linear order, are Susie's words that have nothing to do with any of the mess we have made of things, and nothing to do with choosing between Will and Joe: 'You're not afraid any more.'

*   *   *

In the kitchen, I fill my rucksack with items quickly gathered, scarcely considered: a bottle of water, cold from the fridge, the copy of Plutarch (which I almost leave behind, thinking it somehow wrong to take, and then snatch up anyway), fruit taken from the bowl on top of the fridge, a towel left to dry over the back of a chair. I have just decided that I am ready when I find myself standing quite still, breathing slowly to calm my breathing which is threatening to run wild. Perhaps there is movement at the edge of my vision, or it may be her breathing that alerts my senses to the presence of another. Susie is lying on one of the sofas, one arm above her head and the other trailing on the floor. It is pure luck that I have not woken her. Instead of leaving the room, I find myself staying right where I am, watching her. After a minute, I ease my rucksack off my shoulder, leaving it by the door, and walk across the room. I stand over the sofa. Susie's lips are slightly open and her breathing is gentle and even. Seconds pass and I do not move. It is as if I am waiting for a sign. Then, without stopping to think, I bend over her and place a kiss on her cheek.

Susie's eyelids flicker for a moment. She gives a little intake of breath and then her eyes open.

'Alice?' she says.

I look down at her in silence and then her hand goes to her cheek, her gaze fully awake, never leaving mine. I do not know what I will say, have not planned for this, but Susie seems to understand because she smiles at me and then closes her eyes. A minute later, her breathing is slow again.

I leave her, go back along the hallway to my bedroom door, open it slowly. If he wakes *now*, I think to myself . . . but though the door squeaks slightly on its hinges and light falls into the room from the hallway, Joe does not stir. I sit down on the chair by the door and watch him, just as I watched Susie. Five minutes, I tell myself, but ten minutes and then fifteen minutes pass on my watch-face. Joe sleeps on, nothing disturbing his siesta, and it is strangely mournful, sitting here with him like this. Then elsewhere in the house, I hear a noise. Immediately, I am alert, wondering if Samuel has been dreaming about the sea again and is up already, eager to lose himself in the waves once more. I wait for another minute. The house remains silent. I get up from the chair, open the door and leave the bedroom.

Outside. Behind me the Villa Stamatia does not stir. It is years since I have driven, too scared by the thought of what I might do with all that bunched-up metallic power in my hands, but the steering wheel of the Land Rover is beneath my fingers and the key is in the ignition now and I am turning it. The engine rumbles to life immediately, troubling the still air. I slip the gear stick into reverse easily enough and the car moves backwards, leaving its parking spot in the shade of the trees at the edge of the driveway.

I glance to my right, checking the house one last time. It is then that I see her, watching me from the breakfast terrace. For a moment, my brain is wild, panic-filled, expecting that figure standing there to be Will or Joe, not Susie at all, and then thinking that she has come to stop me, to cause some kind of commotion which will bring the rest of the household running out on to that terrace. I scrabble with the steering wheel, turning the car towards the driveway entrance, but when I look again, she has not moved. Her hand is slowly rising in the air. I watch it, transfixed, not perceiving its meaning at first, and then I understand. We watch one another, Susie and I, across that driveway, the railings of the terrace enclosing her, and her hand stays raised in the air. I hold on tightly to the steering wheel, shape my mouth into a silent goodbye and then my foot finds the accelerator. With a suddenness that startles me, the house is behind me.

The rough dirt track that connects the villa to the coast road sends judders up through the framework of the car, making it lurch a little from side to side. On the back seat, sliding, my rucksack. Beneath an old pair of shorts and a khaki-coloured vest top I am wearing my bikini, and on my feet, a pair of battered canvas trainers which I have owned for ever and which made only the smallest of noises padding across the marbled floor of the villa. I wind down the window. The cicadas throb quietly in the dry undergrowth. The dirt track steepens and I take the Land Rover out of gear, let the car freewheel, fly silently towards the road.

*   *   *

I leave the car outside the travel agency and start out along the quayside, past the rows of yachts, their decks quiet at this hour. A café is open, with a few young Greeks drinking beer at a table. At the far end of the quay the last of the passengers are boarding. I speed up a little, thinking that I will need a minute or two to purchase a ticket, but I am only halfway along that quayside when there is intensified movement and commands being shouted ahead of me and I see that the ferry is about to leave. I break into a trot, a useless kind of half-jog, my rucksack sliding up and down on my back, knowing that I have left it too late, that in a minute's time I will be sitting in the café drinking coffee, contemplating the drive back to the villa. The thought of this overwhelms me. Catching that ferry suddenly becomes huge in my mind. Abandoning any notions of dignity, I stretch out my legs and start to run.

'Wait!' I shout, as I run along the quayside, towards the ferry, but the passengers are all up on deck and the boat is already inching away from shore. A man on the quayside sees me coming, calls something in Greek, and I am sure that I am going to stop, enquire whether there is another ferry I could catch, later in the day, but my legs keep on carrying me towards the stern of that ferry, from where the gangplank has just been removed, towards that expanse of water that is opening up between here and there. The man sees my pace increasing, puts out a hand to stop me, shouts something to a young crew member who, only seconds ago, had been helping passengers on board, and then I know that I am really going to do it and suddenly I am *really* running, sprinting towards that receding point with a tumultuous feeling, on the edge of falling forwards, tumbling back into myself. The man on the quayside grabs for me as I pass but I am ready for him, his shout in my ear, the strong hand I manage to evade. I look ahead, see the startled eyes of the young crew member who understands what I am about to do and is fearful for me, gather up all my strength, push down through the soles of my feet, the balls of my feet, and then leap into nothingness.

*   *   *

The ferry swings around the headland, easing its way out of the bay in which the little village sits into open water. I had promised myself that I would not look, but when it comes to it I cannot help myself. Logic assures me that no one would think to look this way or, what's more, be able to identify me from such a distance. Still I imagine myself exposed by the harsh rays of the sun, which pick me out from this crowd like a spotlight. I play safe, move away quickly from the port bow to shelter behind two black-clad Greek grandmothers who have settled themselves on the fixed wooden seating in the centre of the deck, one of them working a needle through some lace article that falls in delicate folds across her ample lap, the other making steady inroads into a family-size packet of potato chips. It will be coming into view any moment now from behind that stand of cypress trees. The Villa Stamatia.

I try to stare straight ahead, down the wide channel of water that divides this island from its nearest neighbour. Ahead of us, a little pile of clouds, suspended high against the blue sky, the first I have seen since we arrived here. Their edges are strongly delineated, have a purposeful look about them, and I wonder if Alexia was mistaken in her forecast. I glance back towards our bay but keep my gaze down near the shoreline, look towards the house where Michaelis's grandmother lives. An air-force-blue car sits outside. The taxi perhaps, come to take them to the airport. I focus ahead again but the Villa Stamatia will not let me go as easily as that. My eye is inexorably drawn, to the empty beach on our side of the bay and then up the pathway until it disappears into the olive groves which from here seem to hug the land closely, a tenacious mossy carpet. The grey stone of the pool terrace is just there, jutting out slightly like a broken bone, and I can see the pool itself, a blue unnatural glimmer. No movement though.

But there! Before the Villa Stamatia itself, its yellow walls rising square and true from the stony land, the ivy which has begun to encroach upon those clean spaces anchoring it to the earth, *there* is movement. I screw up my eyes; raise my hand to block out the hot glare of the sun which bounces up from the sea. Out here the water moves differently, like dark ropes beneath a glazed surface. I blink, try again, but the heat of the day is pulling up a haze from the island. It rises like a breath from the trees, from the cracked earth. I see – or did I imagine it? – a flash of blue and for a moment I wonder whether I misunderstood Susie this morning, whether she was still hoping – standing out there on the breakfast terrace as I left – that I might rescue her. I feel a pang of misgiving, the old guilt rising because once again I have failed her, proved that there was nothing I could do. The figure separates into two people – walking across what must be the driveway, but no matter how much I narrow my eyes, blink again, I am at too much of a distance. I cannot discern shapes, recognise a particular gait.

They will know by now, have thought little of it at first, until someone noticed the car missing from its place. No one will have thought to look this way though. I had considered leaving a note, propping it up against the coffee pot where it would be sure to be found, but in the end had decided against it, wanting this journey to be unmapped.

The captain shouts something to another member of crew from the little box with Perspex screens on three sides of it – like something a child might build – that serves as a bridge. The boat changes course a little and navy-blue waves slap against the sides in mild protest. We are no longer quite hugging the coastline but peeling away, out towards the middle of the channel, towards Ithaka, and as we do so the feeling of guilt begins to lift a little. It is cooler out here, away from the shore, but if you started to think about it too much, you might still find it hard to breathe. The little bank of clouds has darkened the edge of the sun, but still it is as heavy as brass on my shoulders, my bare thighs. People come up from below deck, where there is no air-conditioning, wiping sweat from their brows and carrying cans of drink and snacks from the small bar. Greek families, the odd day-tripper, an Orthodox priest – all looking for seats. I give up my seat to a mother with a newborn baby and move forward, closer to the prow of the boat, where I ignore the seating provided and wedge myself in beside a small lifeboat. With my tanned skin and my scruffy clothes, I could be mistaken for a backpacker.

A member of crew, the same boy who helped me to my feet when I landed, scrabbling, on the deck of this boat, makes his way forward. He can be no more than twenty but has already learnt that ancient grace peculiar to the Greek sailor. I smile at him, signalling my gratitude once more, and then lean back against the lifeboat, feel the heart of the boat thrumming up through my bones, watch as the Greek boy finally gets past the milling passengers to the prow of the ferry. He shields his eyes and looks ahead towards Ithaka, seeing in that wide blue ocean a course invisible to the rest of us. I turn away from him, crane my neck one last time, looking back at the Villa Stamatia.

It is small from here and the haze is melting its hard, certain edges: a little stage set vaporising in the heat. For a moment I wonder how it could have been, these last few weeks, that its concerns, its happenings came to seem so significant. Then, seeing the Orthodox priest sit down on a bench opposite me and begin unwrapping bread and cheese from a foil package, I realise that I am hungry. I reach into my rucksack and my hand first finds and then closes around something unfamiliar: some kind of object, flexible, smooth-surfaced, laid across the top of the items I packed earlier. I take out what at first seems to be a piece of paper, find that it is a strip of four photographs, like one of the many – now disappeared, forgotten – that Susie and I had taken when we were young. I shade it from the light with my free hand, smile to myself as I remember the photo booth in Woolworths on Daycliffe High Street where we used to arrange ourselves on a regular basis, driven to create a record of ourselves, which was not so much – I am trying to recall the impetus behind our actions – for our own benefit, though we stuck these strips to our bedroom mirrors, to our walls, but because doing so felt like sending a message to the future, a future that was sure to be interested in us. I look more closely and realise that I am mistaken. This one was not taken in Daycliffe after all. The school uniforms, the rain-dampened hair and something behind the bravado of our expressions give it away, and I remember another photo-booth: Victoria Station; the day we ran away for the first time. I turn the strip of photographs over. On the back, no message, just four kisses, quickly scrawled. I place the strip into a side-pocket of the rucksack where it is less likely to become bent or damaged. Then reaching into the main section of the bag, I find the peach I'd been searching for originally, only slightly bruised from its journey. I lift it to my mouth, bite into it. Flesh gives itself up from the stone and here, on this deck, this peach in my hand, sweet juice running down my arm, I am alone. Before me, another island.

'*Panaghia!*' calls the young Greek boy suddenly. *Mother of God!* Heads turn towards the prow where he stands: sandwiches, crisps hover in the air. The boy is looking up to the skies, towards that small bank of clouds that have now covered the sun. His arms are held in front of him, palms turned upwards, and from above, at last, comes a light, cooling rain.